That's t...
We Met

Also by Sudeep Nagarkar

Few Things Left Unsaid
It Started With a Friend Request

That's the Way We Met

kya life hogi set?

SUDEEP NAGARKAR

RANDOM HOUSE INDIA

First published by Random House India in 2012
Eleventh impression in 2014

Copyright © Sudeep Nagarkar 2012

Random House Publishers India Pvt. Ltd.
7th Floor, Infinity Tower C, DLF Cyber City,
Gurgaon – 122002, Haryana

Random House Group Limited
20 Vauxhall Bridge Road
London SW1V 2SA
United Kingdom

978 81 8400 178 5

Typeset in Adobe Garamond Pro by Eleven Arts

Printed and bound in India by Replika Press Pvt. Ltd

A PENGUIN RANDOM HOUSE COMPANY

To my love, wherever you are at the moment

'Love asks me no questions, and gives me endless support.'

—William Shakespeare

Contents

Prologue

It was late evening when I called my girlfriend Riya several times on her mobile. On my repeated failure to get a response, I sent her a text message hoping she'd respond in time. But she didn't. Thinking she might be busy with regular household chores, I put my mind to rest and got busy with work.

Unable to fully concentrate, I checked my mobile phone again. To my utter dismay, there was still no reply from her. Even though I could sense something fishy, I ignored it, choosing to wait for a few more minutes instead. Placing my phone on the table, I went to the washroom. Suddenly, the phone buzzed. I ran towards the table and grabbed it.

It was an unknown number. I picked up the call immediately.

'Hello, Riya?' I said, my voice betraying my growing fear.

'Good evening, sir. We are calling from Vodafone. Your phone number has been selected for a special offer. Would you…'

Before he could get a chance to finish, I slammed down the phone in anger. My frustration had reached its peak. I wanted to scream my lungs out at the customer care executive, but was not in a mood to argue since I wanted to focus all my energy on finding Riya. I disconnected the call and dialled Riya's number again, but failed to get a response. *Where the hell could she be?* I muttered under my breath.

Left with no option, I decided to go to her flat in Navi Mumbai. I took my bike keys and left home. All through the way, I tried to remain calm, convincing myself that nothing had happened. As I entered the apartment complex, I noticed that her scooty was missing from its usual parking spot. I went upstairs and rang the doorbell. Unable to get a response, I rang the bell again and tried to peek in through the keyhole. I soon concluded that no one was at home and left. I tried searching for her scooty in the entire complex, but was unsuccessful. Throughout my search mission, I kept on calling her incessantly, thinking she might respond.

Feeling dejected, I was on my way back home when I happened to see her scooty parked outside a hospital not far from her place. I brought my bike to a screeching halt and rushed towards the hospital.

Once in, I went straight to the reception desk and enquired, 'Could you please check if you have registered a patient by the name of Riya in your hospital?'

The receptionist must have sensed something was wrong as she immediately opened the register and started searching for Riya's name. I tried to maintain my cool even though I was almost in tears. Keeping my fingers crossed, I closed my eyes for a moment and murmured a short prayer.

'I am sorry, sir. I don't seem to have made any entry by that name,' the receptionist replied in a matter-of-fact tone.

I gave her a feeble smile and turned to leave, only to see Riya's brother walking towards me with a medicine packet in his hand. He swiftly walked by and seemed to be in a hurry.

Before I could call out to him and ask what the hell was happening, he had reached the end of the flight of stairs leading to the first floor.

I went to the receptionist desk again to doubly confirm.

'Please, can you check your database again? The person who just went upstairs is the girl's brother. Which room is he headed towards?'

'Hold on, let me check again,' she said looking for another register. 'Yes, go to room number 306, first floor,' she replied.

'One last thing, can you please tell me who is admitted in that room?' I somehow mustered the courage to ask her.

'A girl named Riya. Sorry, I missed that entry earlier,' she said in an apologetic tone.

I stood there in silence, like the world around me had come crashing down. *Was it something serious? Why she did not inform me?* My head was throbbing with a million unanswered questions.

We had made a solemn promise never to cry if ever such a situation arose. But at that moment I felt myself breaking the promise. How could I control my feelings? I wanted to tell Riya that I would give her anything she needed. Hugs, kisses, anything! *But don't meet me in this glum hospital as a patient.* I could barely move my feet. *What if something terrible had happened to her?* I reached room number 306 and slightly pushed the door ajar. My worst fears came true when I saw Riya lying on the bed. She seemed to be asleep. Her mother was sitting next to her, holding Riya's hand affectionately. At that moment, I was terribly afraid.

'Is she fine?' I asked her Mom who got up from her chair and looked at me with a sombre expression on her face.

She remained quiet for a bit. Not knowing whether she hadn't heard me for real or whether she was choosing to ignore me on purpose, I repeated my question. Before she could answer, I saw Riya make an attempt to open her heavily-sedated eyes. Seeing me, she tried to lift her head up and say something. But looking at the frailty of her condition, I stopped her from doing so, gently stroking her forehead.

'What happened, bachha? I tried calling you so many times. Why didn't you inform me that you were ill?' I desperately wanted to know what was happening.

Riya didn't speak a word but kept crying. I wiped the tears from her face and calmed her down.

'Please tell me what happened?' I continued, 'I am dying each second here.'

She still remained quiet. Her hands lifted the cloth that covered her body.

I stopped dead in my tracks. What I saw before me was a nightmare. Riya's body had been strapped with electrodes and there was an IV drip line going through her wrist. I clutched her hand tightly as tears began to trickle down my cheeks.

'Riya, please tell me what has happened to you?' I pleaded.

Before she could answer, a doctor entered the room, followed closely by Riya's Dad who gave me a look of utter contempt, as is I was a stranger who had barged into their private space. Riya's Mom explained to him that I was her friend who had simply come to enquire about her well-being. Hearing this, he calmed down and glanced at Riya with concern, discussing something in hushed tones with the doctor.

'We will have to shift her to Sanjeevani hospital tomorrow. They can treat her better there,' said the doctor.

Her Dad nodded in agreement and went out with his wife to complete the necessary transfer formalities. Left to ourselves, I cast a glance at Riya. Even though her eyes were closed, she didn't let go of her grip on my hand. I felt insecure. I felt alone.

'Don't worry dear. We all are with you. You will get well soon,' I assured her with all my heart.

Leaving her to rest, I went outside and called Sameer, my close friend. He was the only person whom I could count on in such a situation. I explained to him the gravity of her condition and asked him to reach Sanjeevani hospital as quickly as he could.

Sameer gave me a call once he reached the hospital. He was waiting for me near the parking area and asked me to meet him there.

'I can't understand anything, Sameer. I am out of my mind with worry. I didn't know anything was amiss with her health,' I said to him as we walked towards the lobby.

'Don't worry. It won't turn out to be anything serious. If it was something serious, she would have discussed it with you or at least let you know,' said Sameer trying to calm me down.

All the beloved memories from our time spent together came flashing in front of my eyes and I was overcome with a sudden urge to hear her voice, to see her smile, to hold her in my arms…

Seeing Riya's Mom come walking towards me, I hurriedly wiped my tears and gave a weak smile, assuring her that everything was going to be okay.

'Aditya, Riya is under strict observation. The doctor has given firm instructions that only one person can stay with her. So I request you to go home. Your parents will be worried too.'

'It's okay, Aunty. I will wait. I don't feel like leaving her alone just yet.' I wanted to ask her what really had happened to Riya, but refrained from doing so as I judged from her tense face that it was not the right moment.

In my hurry to reach the hospital, I had come without informing my folks at home. Dad was getting increasingly worried and kept calling me on my mobile. Unable to think of an excuse quick enough, I dodged the calls a few times, but ultimately picked up and told him that I was caught up with work in office and would come home as soon as I finished all pending work.

I was nervous and felt helpless about the situation.

'Aditya, please leave. You can come again in the morning during visiting hours,' her Mom requested me after overhearing our conversation on the phone.

Eventually, Sameer and I left the hospital. Sameer tried his best to divert my mind by talking about other, inconsequential stuff, but he couldn't. Somewhere at the back of my mind, I knew he was pretty tensed as well since he too was a close friend of Riya, but he tried his best to maintain a calm exterior for my sake.

Sleep evaded me that night. I kept looking at the watch, hoping the sun would rise early. A feeling of loneliness slowly engulfed me. When I finally closed my eyes, I was reminded of our long drive along the beach a mere two days back. I could still feel the warmth of her hands around my chest as she clung to me closely. It had been such a perfect evening. And now this!

The Story So Far

The new morning brought with it the painful realization of Riya's absence in my life. The warmth of her hug, her loving presence, all of it was gone.

Without waiting to inform my parents, I rushed out of my house and went straight to the hospital. Opening the door to her room, I saw that there was no one inside. My heart skipped a beat. I was already confused after last night's disaster and this made my situation all the more worse.

I ran towards the reception desk to enquire about Riya.

'Can you tell me in which room is the patient Riya? She was admitted here last night and kept under intense observation.' I gave her all the details and waited impatiently while she called someone to check on it.

'I am afraid you are mistaken, sir. We have no patient by that name here,' the receptionist answered.

'Are you sure? Please check again. I was here last night sitting on that very couch right there with her Mom,' I said, almost yelling at her, but she remained firm.

Where could she possibly be? I thought to myself. *Have*

her folks checked her out of the hospital? On an impulse, I decided to go to her home just to be certain.

I wanted to see her. I wanted to hold her hands and tell her everything was going to be okay. I loved her more than anything in the world and wanted to have a chance to express my emotions at least once to her. I wanted to love her again, wanted to tell her once more that she is mine... just mine, and that no one can separate us. But I felt helpless.

Reaching her apartment, I walked up the stairs with a heavy heart and rang the doorbell. Riya's Mom opened the door. She greeted me and went inside the kitchen. I scanned the room quickly, searching for Riya's familiar presence.

'Aditya, will you have a cup of tea?' Riya's Mom asked me from the kitchen.

Was I up for a cup of tea when I did not know where the love of my life was? I think not. But I politely declined, just wanting to know what was happening.

Suddenly, Riya emerged from her bedroom in the most nonchalant fashion, as if nothing had happened to her. I just stood there in complete silence, looking at her from head to toe, soaking it all in.

'What's wrong, Aadi? What are you doing here? And why do you seem so shocked?' she said firing questions at me.

'I should be asking you the same thing. When did you get discharged from the hospital? And why didn't you inform me even after I repeatedly told you to do so?'

She looked clueless, as is she didn't understand a word I was saying. She came close to me and said, 'What's wrong with you?'

'Nothing's wrong with me. But where were you last night? And why didn't you pick up my call in the morning?' I asked.

'What are you talking about? Of course, I was at home last night. When you called me in the morning, I was taking a bath, so I couldn't pick up your call. And why are you screaming at me? Are you drunk? Don't lie. You haven't even noticed the fragrance of your favourite perfume.'

And then it finally dawned upon me—I had been dreaming! A horrible, horrible dream! I was so deep in sleep that I didn't even realize that all of last night's happenings were just being played out in my dream. *Was work stress, leading to lack of proper sleep, a reason for my delusion?* I asked myself. If I had spoken to my Mom before leaving the house, I would have known better.

I breathed a sigh of relief.

Goodness gracious! Everything I had seen until now, everything I had visualized about the hospital was just that—a dream. I told all this to Riya, who could not stop laughing at my expense.

Finally, I took in the scent of my favourite perfume. Her hair was dripping wet. She was in my favourite colour—a red sequinned blouse paired with a black, knee-length skirt, and a bracelet in her left hand. She looked perfect.

Since our offices were located in the same area, we decided to leave together. I held her by the waist while walking towards my bike. I felt complete. I looked at her—her black eyeliner made her look even more beautiful. She blinked her eyes and smiled.

There are no words to describe her beauty. There are no words to describe how special she or my love for her is. Putting these feelings into words will mean defining it and that would also mean limiting it. The truth is, there is neither a limit nor a definition for love.

'Promise me you will never be out of my sight for so long ever again,' I told her. 'I was so afraid of losing you yesterday.'

'Aadi, not even God can separate us. He brought us together once again so that we could have another chance at love. And I will not let that chance pass.' She gave me a slight peck on the cheek after which we left for work.

The sun had set early that day, leaving short our pleasure of watching the fading twilight. A cold wind blowing from the beach caught us completely by surprise. I could feel the warmth of her body as she clung to me firmly for support on my motorbike. I cast a glance at her through the rear-view mirror and could see the love she had for me in her eyes. I had no faith in destiny before I met her. Riya smiled back at me, her smile symbolic of eternal love.

'Aditya, will you please stop staring at me? Every time you look at me like that, I get goosebumps,' said Riya with a shy smile on her lips.

'I can stare at you my entire life. You are mine, just mine,' I said, kissing her hand.

Our love was meant to be forever and nothing, not even God, could come in the way of that. True love is hard to find, but it's pure, and has a magical power to it. We fought in our early days, we cried, heck, we even broke up! But our love for each other never ceased.

My Karizma cruised comfortably along the long-winding road. The moment she kept her head on my shoulders, I could not resist bending towards her. I wanted to spend my entire life gazing at her beautiful glistening eyes, her pink alluring lips, and her lustrous, glossy hair. I looked at her from the rear-view mirror again and saw that she had closed her eyes. Maybe her hectic office schedule had tired her out. It was a weekday and I had picked her up from her office in Malad. We had decided to have dinner together and had singled out an eatery near her house.

'You look tired. Is everything fine at the office?' I asked her once seated in the restaurant.

'Everything's fine. I had to take back-to-back client calls today and couldn't take my usual break.' She seemed exhausted.

'Oh, my sweetheart,' I said kissing her hand with affection.

We ordered dinner and looked at the other guests seated around us. We noticed a couple fighting at the table adjoining ours. I was trying to eavesdrop on their conversation. Seeing the couple made me remember my early days with Riya when we would endlessly fight over small things.

Both of us looked at each other.

'Are you thinking the same thing as me?' I questioned her.

'Yes. We were idiots. We would fight just like them. Silly reasons that would culminate into stupid arguments,' said Riya taking a bite of the pizza we had ordered.

'You think that we don't fight as much now?'

'Of course we do,' she replied, 'But now we understand each other's emotions way better.'

Life without love is like a scorching desert craving for rain. Riya came in my life and cured all my pain. Our relationship had an inseparable emotional bonding.

I kept looking at her without saying a word.

'Jaan, let's go for a long drive.' I wanted to salvage the little time we had at hand before work beckoned.

'I don't think that's a very good idea. We have to go to office right now, remember? Let's go, please,' she requested.

'Let's wait for a few more minutes, please. I want to feel you in my arms, I want to look deep into your eyes and tell you just how much I love you.'

'You will never change.' She gave a wicked smile, pinching me hard.

I bent forward and gave her a slight peck on her cheek. She responded with equal intensity and planted a gentle kiss on my neck. Her eyes met mine and melted me with its intensity—intensity of an unconditional love that sent shivers down my spine.

'I love you, Riya.' The honest confession was made in that one magical moment.

'I love you too.'

I dropped her to office after our delightful evening together. As I saw her enter the gate of her office building, I thanked my stars for the good fortune of having someone like Riya to love with all my heart.

But somewhere in the corners of our minds, I knew that we still had the fear of losing each other. Neither of us chose to express our concerns to the other for fear of the intuition coming true. Never in my wildest dreams did I think that one person could light up my entire life, that my every decision would require her approval.

I loved Riya. This time more deeply, madly, and passionately.

Haseen pal kissa ban jaata hai,
Koi shaks apna hissa ban jaata hai,
Kuch log aise milte hain,
Jinse kabhi na tootne waala rishta ban jata hai.

The 'M' factor

I was scheduled to attend a conference meet in my office where managers were addressing agent-level employees.

'Your team needs to work on your Net Sat (Net Satisfaction of the Customer) score. The quarterly figures for your group are extremely poor,' said the manager, almost yelling at our team in the conference room.

Sitting way behind all the rest, cleverly shielded from the manager, I was busy texting Riya from my cell phone. She didn't seem to be working as was evident in her quick replies.

'I strictly want all of you to follow the official dress code! No one should wear casuals on weekdays. Moreover, on Monday, everyone should come dressed in black office formals. Recently, I have been getting repeated complaints from the HR team that some you are violating certain company policies regarding the established dress code. Strict action will be taken against anyone found breaching the desired code of conduct. The guidelines for proper dressing will shortly be put up on the bulletin board. Remember, casual dressing is allowed only on Fridays,' he yelled at our team, even though I don't think anyone was really paying heed to what he had to say.

All that screaming was proving to be too much of an overdose for me. I desperately needed a smoke. No wonder I hated managers. *They are utter morons. Where do they get the energy to speak so much?*

'Why don't you just take all your traditional beliefs about organizations and apply them to the neurons in your brains?' he continued.

I wanted to stand up and tell him that Rome wasn't built in a day, so how could he expect us to remember all the guidelines in a matter of a few days? After all, the new dress code policy had been introduced only recently. I waited for him to stop laying all that crap on us and give us a breather.

As the meeting wrapped up, I hastily left the room and went straight to the smoking zone where I lit a cigarette and breathed out a relieved puff.

'Hey, how are you?' I heard someone say from behind me. I turned back and saw Prerna, my colleague from the same division.

'Plain fucked up! We had a meeting with the managerial team and they screwed us as usual. But anyway, how have you been?' I replied.

We then broke into a general discussion on our 'not so happening' corporate life. As the five-minute break was just about to get over, I told her to meet me in the next break to continue with our rant.

I was just logging into my system when the team manager showed up. He introduced us to our new team leader, Mohit, who had joined us from our regional office in Ahmedabad. He had recently been transferred to Mumbai and had been asked to resume duties in our office. Mohit was smartly dressed and even though he seemed young, he had the look of someone with years of experience behind him. He gave us a warm smile and individually greeted everyone with a handshake. We then resumed work with Mohit keeping a close watch on us, ready to guide us through any improbable complications.

After an hour had eloped, I locked my system and went outside for a short break. Prerna was in the smoking zone before me.

'How is Riya?' she asked. Everyone in my close network of friends knew about my relationship with Riya.

Before I could answer, Mohit came in and asked me for a lighter. I took out one from my pocket and lit his cigarette. That seemed to break the ice between us. Mohit was the first one to ask me, 'Aditya, were you born and brought up in Mumbai?'

I replied in the affirmative.

'Great! I'm staying in a hotel as of now. But since I will be working here for good, I wanted to look for a permanent accommodation. Since it is my first time in the city, Mumbai is an alien land for me and I don't know my way around here. Do you know of any decent place where I could shift?'

'But I thought our company was providing you with accommodation?' I asked with a surprised look. Usually, whenever we had inter-city transfers, the company usually took it upon itself to provide the employees with proper accommodation.

'Yes, they will, but only after two months. Till that time, I was looking for a room on rent, preferably some place within my budget and which his close to our company,' said Mohit.

'I can put you in touch with my friend who rents out flats. Plus, I won't charge you much or take commission,' I winked.

'That makes things much easier for me. Thanks a lot, Aditya. I owe you one.'

Mohit shifted to the apartment suggested by my friend the very next day.

He was single which was hard to believe, since he was quite a pretty good-looking guy, or so I could tell from the way girls cast a glance at him every time he passed by. His family was based in Ahmedabad where he had spent most of his formative years. We became good friends soon after.

It was another office day and Mohit and I had been slogging it out.

'Do you have a girlfriend?' asked Mohit while accompanying me to the gate after our shift got over.

'Yes. Her name is Riya. We have been seeing each other since the past few years.'

'Are you guys planning to get married soon?'

I could feel myself go red in the face. Even though we loved each other deeply, marriage was not on the cards—at least for me.

'Yes, maybe three years from now we will. Anyway, it's too early for me to answer this,' I smiled as I lit a cigarette.

'Mohit, Riya is on her way to meet me. If you aren't too busy, would you care to join us?' I casually asked him.

Like I expected, he politely declined. But I insisted he should wait so that I could at least introduce Riya to him. By the time we inhaled our last puffs, Riya joined us in the parking lot. I introduced both of them with each other.

'It's great to finally meet you, Riya. I have heard so much about you. In fact, we were just talking about you. I was asking Aditya about his marriage plans and he told me he was confused,' said Mohit with a mischievous twinkle in his eyes.

'Did you, Aditya? Don't pay any heed to him, Mohit. We will get married one day, just not anytime soon' said Riya.

'Aditya, you are one lucky chap,' he said patting me on my back.

I held Riya by the waist and said, 'Isn't she equally lucky?'

Both of them nodded in agreement. We then headed to the Cafe Coffee Day outlet near our office. Once we were seated comfortably, I told Riya how good she looked in her trousers and white top—a corporate look that particularly flattered her beauty. Her hair fell loosely on her shoulders and she gave me a perfect smile in exchange for my compliment. I saw myself falling for her all over again.

'So guys, do your parents know about your relationship?' Mohit asked while taking a sip of his cappuccino.

We looked at each other and answered at the same moment, 'NO'.

Even though my Mom had some sort of inkling about our relationship, Riya's Mom thought we were best friends who simply chose to hang out together quite often.

'You both look good together,' Mohit stated.

'Isn't it amazing how a person who was once a stranger suddenly becomes your world?' I asked as Riya kissed my cheek.

'Yes it is. And it is nice to know that love like yours still exists in the world,' Mohit continued.

'So let's turn the tables on you, Mohit. When are you planning to settle down?' I asked.

I told Riya that he was single which she found hard to believe.

'You can date Prerna, you know. She is a real hottie with a body to die for,' I teased Mohit. Riya pinched me on my arm and gave me a disapproving look.

'Shut up and stop kidding! Let's get going,' said Mohit getting up from his seat.

Arching one eyebrow, Riya signalled me to stay back and let Mohit go. Mohit understood that we wanted to be left alone for sometime. He excused himself and took the bus back home while we zoomed off on my bike.

'So what do you think about getting married?' I casually asked Riya while driving down to Marine Drive.

'Aadi, you know I want to marry you—I have ever since I met you. But I want to become financially stable before that. You know how I feel about living off someone else's money.'

I did not want to spoil our evening, so I chose to remain silent on the issue and dropped her off near her house. How was I to know that it would become a major bone of contention between us later on?

Mumbai Rains

It had been one helluva long day. But since it was a Friday, the weekend was thankfully just round the corner. And the temptation of the approaching weekend made it impossible to concentrate on work. I wanted to complete my target for the day on time and leave. Mohit came and monitored my last call before pack up.

'Thank you for calling SGS. How may I help you?' I asked in a mechanical tone opening my call.

'Listen, I am facing difficulty logging onto the internet,' the customer complained.

'What is the error message on your computer screen?' I looked at Mohit. He instructed me to keep a track on the AST (Average Session Time).

'The prompt that I am getting is "wrong user ID/password",' he grunted.

'Can I confirm that you are keying in your password with the Caps Lock key off?' I asked.

'What is that all about?'

'Sir, I think you need to type in your password in lowercase after turning off your Caps Lock key. Would you do that and let me know if it works?' I suggested.

'Look here, this is bullshit! There is no such thing as switching off the Caps Lock—I can't do that.' the customer said in an agitated voice. Watching the proceedings behind my desk, Mohit was trying his best to control his laughter.

'Why don't you give it a try, sir? Just press your caps lock key and you will get a prompt on the right hand corner of your screen saying "caps lock key off". Then punch in your password. If it still doesn't work, we can try something else,' I said in a mock serious tone.

'Oh my God, you are right! I had been typing the password in capital letters all along! Dude, you are a fucking genius,' he muttered in excitement. *And dude, even a child would have been able to figure it out*, I thought to myself.

Once I hung up the phone after giving him a lowdown on all the basics, I burst out laughing, joined soon by Mohit who still seemed pretty amused by it.

A happy customer meant an increase in my Net Sat score. I logged off the system and left the floor with Mohit who wanted to know my weekend plans and suggested we hang out together if I wasn't pre-engaged in another thing. Since I didn't have any concrete plans as such, I agreed to meet him on Saturday. Then I rushed to meet Riya after my shift.

Once seated at our regular meeting point—a dhaba outside her office—she asked me, 'What are you doing tomorrow? Let's go out somewhere.'

I couldn't tell her outright that I had already made plans with Mohit, but I also did not want to say no to her. So I made up a miserable excuse of having some pending office work. She didn't say anything but her face told me she was clearly upset. I knew she wasn't buying it. I thought for a moment and said, 'Okay, I will try and finish all pending work on Sunday. But can Mohit also join us tomorrow? He is new to the city and wanted help exploring it. Plus, it's more fun in a group. We could all just aimlessly roam around the city. And I am sure you must now be bored by my company. What do you think?'

She didn't say anything for a while. Then she smiled and I knew she had fallen for it.

'What if Sonam also joins us?' Riya suggested.

'That's perfect. That'll allow us to have some time for our own without feeling guilty about Mohit getting bored since he will have Sonam for company,' I added.

Sonam was Riya's good friend and colleague. A Delhi girl, she lived with her relatives in Mumbai. I told Mohit about our double date and asked if he was comfortable with the plan. At first he hesitated, but finally gave in after I pestered and reminded him what a head turner Sonam was. We decided to meet at Inorbit Mall in Malad at 1 pm.

I messaged Riya that night:

Babe, I was just thinking about our college days and how much fun we had together. Remember how you used to force me to write long messages even though I could barely write a sentence? I used to send you the same forwarded messages over and over again. But it's different today. Now words aren't enough to tell you how wonderful you are. Although this is just a small attempt to do so, the fact that will remain constant is that I will love you forever. Here's a love message that was in my inbox which I had saved to send you at the apt moment. 'I wish I was your blanket, I wish I was your bed; I wish I was your pillow underneath your head. I want to be around you, I want to hold you tight and be the lucky person who kisses you good night.'

Riya replied:

Aadi, I don't need fancy love messages to assure me of your love. You are a blessing in disguise to me. I cherish every second I spend with you. I find myself loving you more with each passing day. You are the reason for my being. You are my Mr Perfect and I love you.

I slept with a smile on my face that night.

I reached Malad at 1 pm sharp and spotted Sonam sitting near the water fountain. She was wearing a white halter-neck top with dark blue slim-fit jeans. Mohit and Riya were yet to arrive. I greeted her with a casual 'hello'. After a few minutes, Riya arrived. I was amazed at how she could take my breath away every time I glanced at her. She was suitably dressed for the hot weather in a blue tube top and shorts which showed off her perfectly toned legs. She was wearing the blue bracelet that I had gifted her on her last birthday on her right wrist. She came close to me and gave me a slight peck on my cheek. I whispered to her how beautiful she looked. Before she could get a chance to reply, we saw Mohit enter from the mall's main gate. Riya introduced Mohit to Sonam. We chilled out in the mall for a while, after which we decided to start our Mumbai tour from Bandra.

We hopped into my car, with Riya sitting in the front with me while Mohit and Sonam sat in the backseat.

'Sonam, even you have never explored the city or so I hear from Riya? I was under the impression that it has been quite a while since you came to Mumbai,' I asked her.

'Not really. In my line of work, we hardly get weekends off and when we do, I prefer to stay at home and get some rest,' said Sonam.

'Your job must suck then! So listen up guys—what I propose is that we go to Bandstand first and then head off to the Gateway of India. Does that sound good?' I asked. Everyone seemed to like the idea.

We reached Bandstand within an hour. I parked my car near Taj Lands End hotel. Mohit's excitement on seeing the sea was visible on his face. We walked towards the seashore. The girls were walking ahead of us, deep in conversation like teenage school girls who had lots to gossip about. I observed Mohit glancing at Sonam. It made me smile.

'This is Bandstand, the most famous lover's point in Mumbai. Mannat adds to its charm,' said Riya.

'Mannat is Shahrukh Khan's house, right?' Sonam asked curiously.

'Yes. It's on that side of the road. Let's walk and see if we can click some snaps,' I said as we walked towards Mannat. 'Maybe we can spot Shahrukh too,' said Riya

Sonam and Mohit turned out to be huge Shahrukh Khan fans and were equally excited to click snaps in front of the now world-famous bungalow. Mohit peeped inside the huge gate but could see nothing except for a couple of seemingly expensive cars. Mohit cheekily went up to the security guard and asked if Shahrukh was at home. However, the security guard shooed us away. I clicked many pictures of Mohit and Sonam near the bungalow. Then Mohit took the camera from me and forced Riya and me to pose together. After our photo session was over, we headed back towards the seashore.

I rummaged for a cigarette in my pocket. Seeing me light one, Riya screamed like a possessive housewife, saying, 'How many times have I told you not to smoke when I am with you?' Sonam too gave me a disapproving look.

'I will, someday. But that someday is not today, love. Now please let me smoke,' I pleaded with her.

I looked at Mohit and to my surprise, he slyly put back his cigarette in his pocket. Mohit was a heavy smoker and I had seen him openly smoke in office. So I found his action a bit odd. But then it struck me—he was trying to impress Sonam! Maybe he was warming up to her and did not want to put her off with his smoking habit on the very first day of their meeting.

We sat on a bench, feeling the cold breeze from the sea lightly kiss our faces. Riya snuggled up to me, resting her head on my shoulder. I kissed her hand and told her how beautiful she was for the umpteenth time.

I could envision another love story in the making with Sonam and Mohit deeply engrossed in conversation on another bench. Riya and I left them alone and went near the seashore.

'You look amazing today. Or wait, I have told that to you already, right? I get so jealous and insecure when people turn around and look at you,' I said. The look that passersby gave her clearly hadn't gone unnoticed by me—call me possessive.

'Oh c'mon, Aadi! You know I am all yours. No one can take me away from you. You know that very well,' said Riya trying to dispel my jealousy.

We walked hand in hand for a few miles, and Riya kept picking up pebbles that had been washed away by the sea waves. We walked on the beach, watching the sifting sand beneath our feet and the swirling salty water washing away a footprints.

Content with spending time with each other, we went back to where we had left Mohit and Sonam before starting our little sojourn down the beach. Both were seated in exactly the same position we had left them in, deeply rooted in conversation. Looking at them, no one would have guessed that it was their first meeting. Their body language expressed how comfortable they were in each other's company.

We chose to silently watch them from a distance. Mohit seemed to be telling Sonam a funny story since all she did was throw her head back in laughter. Then we saw a man approaching Mohit and ask for a cigarette.

'Hi, may I know your name?' the man asked Mohit.

'Mohit,' he replied. I could tell he was feeling a little uncomfortable seeing the uninvited man barge into their private space.

I sized up the man from head to toe. He looked unsuitably dressed for an evening on the beach—like he was going to a party. He was wearing tight blue jeans with an odd-looking shirt that could easily pass off as a woman's top. His hand gestures seemed unusual too.

'Are you from Mumbai?' he asked Mohit.

Was he a cop? I asked myself. His dressing and peculiar mannerisms certainly didn't make it seem so.

'I am from Ahmedabad but I work in Mumbai,' Mohit answered.

'If you don't mind me saying it, you are quite a good-looking guy. And I think you have a great physique too. That's a lethal combination,' he said.

Oh dear Lord, where is this conversation headed? I sensed he was gay. However, I chose to keep my observations to myself for the time being.

'If you have a bit of time to spare, could I talk to you for a few minutes?' he continued. I don't know why Mohit agreed to go with him but he did. Maybe he wanted to have a few laughs by himself or could not read into the man's overtures.

We joined Sonam and all three of us tried our best to eavesdrop on their conversation.

'Sonam, is Mohit gay?' I whispered.

'Shut up! He is not. Or not that I know of till now,' Sonam said.

'How do you know?' I joked.

'Let's just say I have a sense about these things.'

'Oh do you? Tell me, did he kiss you or give some sort of signal to prove that he is not gay?' I said pulling her leg.

'I will kill you someday, Aadi! You will never change,' she said, trying her best to ignore my teasing.

I laughed and looked at Riya. She glowered. I apologized and told her I was joking. Mohit came back with a blank expression on on his face. We were eager to know what had transpired between the two of them. *Was he gay or was he a cop?* In my mind, the probability of the former seemed more. I couldn't wait to know and almost pounced on Mohit with my questions.

'That bastard, he was a gay! He asked me to give him company for the night and also said he would pay me two thousand rupees for doing so. I was dumbstruck by the revelation and by his offer. How could he think I would entertain such a baseless idea? Do I look gay from any angle? I wanted to run away at once, but instead excused myself by making up some petty excuse and came here.'

'What did you say?' Riya asked.

'Does that really matter when the guy almost had half his mind of taking me to bed and raping me?' said Mohit dumbfounded.

'How did you tear away from his arms?' I laughed.

'I'll kick your ass, Aditya. I swear. I wish you were in my place to realize how humiliated I feel,' he continued, 'I told him I was impotent.'

We looked at each other and burst out laughing. Mohit glared at us for sometime, but finally gave in and joined in the laughter.

The four of us laughed all through our way to the Gateway of India. We had drinks and lunch at Café Mondegar, a restro bar famous for its waffles, pancakes, and a jukebox that belts out jazz music. We were having a ball and in all the revelry, it was easier to forget that Mohit was my team leader. Riya seemed to be in a perky mood as she kept tickling my feet under the table all through lunch. We teased Mohit and Sonam for most part of the meal. Doing that reminded me of how my friends would tease Riya and me the same way during our first few dates.

On an impulse, I broke into a song, '*Tujhe dekh dekh sona, tujhe dekh kar hai jagnaa, maine ye zindagani sang tere bitaani, tujhme basi hai meri jaan haaye, Jiya dhadak dhadak, dhadak dhadak jaaye.'* Everyone seemed to be having a good time.

After a splendid lunch, we decided to go for a short walk near the Taj Hotel.

'Just looking at the hotel reminds me of the horrifying incident of the 26/11 terror attacks here. It was indeed a black day!' said Mohit looking at the Taj.

'You know, I had a close brush with death that day. I was in Café Mondegar with Sameer at around 7 pm the day the terrorists struck the city. I had received my first paycheck and we had decided to go to the café to celebrate. A couple of beers down, I suggested we eat dinner at the Taj since I wanted to blow my first paycheck in style. But we eventually dropped the plan and went to Koylas instead, which is a nice eatery near Mondegar. Suddenly, we saw a group of police officers enter the restaurant. They told us the hotel was under siege due to a terrorist threat and warned us not to leave the restaurant without permission. We could hear the deafening sound of gun blasts all around us but the cops did not allow us to move out. That day we saw death with our very eyes. It was just terrible.'

'My God, Aditya! That must have been quite an ordeal. I can understand how you must have felt at that moment. I got goosebumps simply by hearing you talk about it,' said Mohit.

'It angers me to see our government taking things so lightly. Even though a terrorist has been captured, the bastard is yet to be legally punished.'

'The government just makes a fool of us. Who knows how far they are telling the truth? We simply follow what media covers. The inside story is always shrouded in mystery,' said Sonam.

'All we can do on our part is pray for the ones who lost their lives,' I continued.

'I feel sad for for the foreigners who were specifically targeted. It's just such a cheap act and our cops were totally helpless about it,' Riya added.

'But we must not forget that they tried their best to counter the terrorists. Heck, our three officers even lost their lives in the process. We can just pray for the victims and their bereaved families and keep our fingers crossed that the terrorists won't attack us now,' I said trying to lighten up the situation.

We took pictures of the Taj and then walked towards the Gateway of India where we chanced upon an astrologer sitting at one corner. Even though I didn't believe in superstitions, I gave in, thinking it would be fun to have our future predicted as all of us were together. Riya went ahead and showed him her palm.

'You will get married to someone wealthy and someone who is a distant member of your family,' he said looking at my hand.

Riya looked at me and smiled. He then continued with his predictions and said, 'It will be an arranged marriage.'

Riya didn't say anything to him and got up. Mohit was up next.

'Your wife will be from the northern part of India. You will be extremely happy with her and will most likely get engaged this year,' he said.

I looked at Mohit who in turn looked at Sonam. She blushed in embarrassment. They didn't say anything to each other.

Riya got angry at me for having brought us to this fake astrologer. She believed it was a complete waste of time on our part. We paid the astrologer and moved away. Mohit and Sonam went to devour a plate of pani puri while Riya and I chose to sit by the edge of the rocks, holding hands and watching the fading sunset together.

'Meeting you was pure destiny. You and I were always meant to be together. Sitting here and watching the sun go down with you for company, what more could I ask for? All I desire is to be able to watch every sunset with you till death does us apart,' I told Riya earnestly, giving her one last kiss before the sun faded away for the day.

We got back to Mohit and Sonam who seemed to be enjoying each other's company thoroughly. Then we took off from the Gateway of India and drove towards Marine Drive, which is believed to be the most romantic place in Mumbai, especially after sunset.

We went for a buggi ride and feasted on chaat and chuskis. Riya had a particular favourite food joint in Marine Drive called Bachelor's Snacks Corner which was famous for its chilli ice-cream. It was the perfect way to mark the end of a grand day. We drove our car near Marine Drive, playing music on full blast. Sonam and Riya grooved to the sound of the music.

When I sneaked a glance at Riya, she gave me a wink and kept her hand on my palm which was changing gears. I was caught completely unawares and the tingle of her touch made it difficult for me to drive. Not that I wanted her to remove her hand.

Since it was a beautiful night, we made a spontaneous decision of walking on foot for a few kilometres. I parked the car in one corner before we got down. We walked on the edge of the road watching the waves disappear. Sonam and Mohit walked ahead of us. Riya and I could tell that they were getting increasingly close to each other, but were refraining from expressing their feelings.

When Mohit and Riya were at quite a distance from us, Riya whispered to me, 'I want to get naughty with you.'

'I will kill you! Stop it! We are in a public place,' I retorted. She came close to me. I played with a few loose strands of her hair and inhaled her scent. We broke into a close hug as the powerful waves crashed against the rocks. Out of the blue, a sudden downpour broke our hug. Just as I was getting up to run for cover, Riya pulled me back and brought me close to her—stopping me from taking shelter. We were completely drenched within a few minutes.

'Riya, it's raining heavily. You will fall ill. Let's move from here,' I pleaded.

'It is getting romantic and you want to leave? How unromantic! Stop behaving like a kid and enjoy the rain with me,' she said, wrapping her hands around me.

I took the cue and came and sat right next to her. I wanted to feel this magical moment together. The grey sea and the long black land, the yellow half-moon and the startled waves added to the romance. As the moon shone upon us, bathing us in its glowing light, I glanced at Riya's eyes and kissed them. Then we engaged in a long, passionate kiss.

'If you get a chance to go back and change one thing in our relationship, what will that be?' Riya asked.

'There is nothing I'd want to change, except realize my dream to dance with you in the rain. We never got a chance to do that, but today we can. Will you dance with me?'

'Here, by the road? I can't,' she said shyly.

'There is no one around, not even Mohit and Sonam. Let's make our dream come true.'

I pulled Riya in my arms and we started dancing. I held her waist and she put her head on my shoulder. We hummed softly and slowly moved our feet to the song playing on my mobile phone. Neither of us had any sort of formal training in dance, but who gave a damn about training when the person you loved was dancing in your arms? The wind blew our hair and the sound of the waves added rhythm to our dance. Riya closed her eyes and told me how much she was enjoying herself.

'Ahem, ahem…guys, time to break the party. My God, you both seem fully drenched in the rain,' said Mohit interrupting us.

'Where were you both? I thought you had completely forgotten that we existed,' I exaggerated a little to save my ass. Sonam could have killed me there itself. But to my surprise, she smiled.

'We wanted to give you guys some privacy. So we chose to go for a long walk,' said Sonam.

'I knew you would come up with a silly excuse for being alone with Sonam. Try something new. It's perfectly okay if you wanted some "alone time" with him, you don't need to hide your emotions for that,' I said cheekily. I loved irritating Sonam.

Mohit started speaking in Sonam's defence and I could sense they liked each other. We got in the car to leave as it was getting increasingly late. I dropped Riya off first, in an effort to get her home before her curfew, followed by Sonam and Mohit.

As soon as I reached home, I got a message from both Riya and Mohit:

Thanks, Aditya. Not just for making my day memorable by hanging out with me, but also for fixing me up with Sonam, even though I was not too sure of it at first. I think I really like her. Please don't mention any of this to her yet, since I want to be positively sure about it myself. And I also don't know if she likes me or not. I don't want to force her into liking me or getting into a relationship with me. I don't even know if she is committed to someone else. Don't know if I am making any sense to you. Let's talk about this on Monday. Bye.

I instantly sent him a reply:

Sure. I think Sonam likes you too. See you on Monday.

The second was a message from Riya:

After a long time, I thoroughly enjoyed the day. I loved the way you danced with me. You have a real romantic side to you and I love you for that. You are the best boyfriend and if I may add so, an awesome kisser as well. I loved each moment with you today. Can we go out again tomorrow? The place doesn't matter as long as I am with you. I want to spend this Sunday with you before my boring work beckons. I want to bring back the memories of our past when we would spend the entire day together. Let me know if you are game for it?

I replied:

Hey, now that's a coincidence. I was just about to ask you to go out on a date with me tomorrow when I saw your message. Let's make tomorrow's date even more special than today's. By the way, Mohit messaged me saying he likes Sonam. But he has told me to not tell Sonam about it, so you don't either.

As I lay my head on the pillow, I could still feel her body close to mine when we danced together in the rain. I slept thinking of her—my angel.

A Splashful Day

After a good night's sleep, I woke up feeling perky. The plan was to meet at Water Kingdom, Asia's largest water park. Once there, we obtained rented swimsuits from one of the shops. Riya looked smouldering hot in her swimming outfit which clung to her curves in all the right spots. Once out of our respective changing rooms, I planted a kiss on her forehead. Pulling her close to me, I said, 'I will never leave you.'

'I am the luckiest girl in the world to have you in my life, Aditya.' We held hands and walked together to the wave pool.

'Come jaan!' I called Riya over to join me while she was still at the shallow end of the pool. She refused to budge saying that she feared swimming in the deep end. But I assured her that she was safe in my arms and gestured her to come to me.

'No,' she said panicking and tried to push my hands away. But I was a bit too strong for her lean body.

Just as she managed to escape through my clutches, the waves hit us, toppling her over me. I grabbed her waist and gripped it tightly so that she had no room to escape. The waves carried us high in the air and dropped us back with a splash, spraying water on our faces and causing us to choke.

'Let's get back to the shallow end,' said Riya trying to break free from my grip.

'If I let go, you will drown. See.' I removed my hands from her waist and she was about to drift away with the waves when I rescued her just in time. I started laughing loudly. Realizing that she had been fooled, she started splashing water on me. I knew that I had taken the joke too far, so I went close to her and gave her a tight hug. She hit me slightly on the chest as a punishment for my act. I squeezed cheeks lightly, apologizing profusely for having taken advantage of her fear. Then we enjoyed a few dry rides and grabbed a quick bite at Mc Donald's. While Riya waited in line to place her order, I got a call from Mohit who updated me on his heart state of affairs.

'What did Mohit say?' asked Riya digging into the burger a few minutes later.

'He told me he really likes Sonam and that he has never felt like this about anyone before. It seems like they got talking yesterday and really hit it off. He doesn't know for sure whether Sonam likes him or not, but he is willing to take this forward and give it a shot. And if my hunch is correct, I think Sonam likes him too. The fact that she willingly gave Mohit her number before leaving last night clearly hints at the fact that she is interested.'

'I couldn't agree more. Come to think of it, Sonam did ask me many questions about him last night. I think they will really make a cute couple. I hope it works out between them,' Riya prayed.

We finished our meal and when we came out, I gave Riya a surprise gift wrapped in coloured paper.

'What is it?' she asked curiously, slowly unwrapping the gift. It was a greeting card on the envelope of which I had meticulously stuck rose petals.

'Oh my God, Aditya. It's beautiful,' she said hugging me.

'Wait till you see what's on the inside,' I told her.

She carefully opened the envelope and brought out the card. There she saw a small collage of our photographs pasted on the front cover with an accompanying note inside which said:

I am so lucky to have found you, Riya. I feel such joy when we sit on the couch and talk. My heart is at peace when we lie down on the floor and cuddle. I get immense pleasure from gently touching your face and feel tremendous passion when I touch your lips. I love holding your hand across the table at a restaurant or while walking together.

Our love has been assaulted many times and I am convinced that it is true because the longer I am away from you, the greater is my yearning to be with you once again. You are my enchanted Princess, and I am your devoted Prince.

You honour the man I am, rather than trying to make me someone I am not. I love you because you appreciate me, complete me.

She stood there stunned for a while, trying to take it all in. But her eyes said everything. Then she gave me a big hug. The crowd was gawking at our public display of affection but we couldn't have bothered less. Today, she didn't care at all.

'Why are you staring at me? Kiss me, you fool,' said Riya puckering up in full public view.

And what a kiss it was! We stood there embarrassed afterwards, feeling a bit tipsy from the long kiss.

My mind raced back to the time when I had first proposed to her. I asked her if she had any memory of it.

'How can I forget that, Aadi? That was one of the best moments of my life and I'll cherish it forever,' said Riya.

We then decided to go to the rain dance section. They had a professional DJ who was belting out the latest hits, perfect for us to dance on. We got onto the dance floor as the lights dimmed and added to the romantic ambience. Riya took my hands and locked them around her tiny waist. As we swirled, I lifted her up from the ground—liberating two souls in love.

The DJ was now entertaining requests for specific songs, so I climbed onto the dais to dedicate one to Riya. Taking the mic from his hand, I said, 'I love you Riya and I want to be with you for the rest of my life. I want to apologize for all the times that I have hurt you. Trust me, it wasn't done intentionally. What I love about you the most is your spirit of generosity and forgiveness. You never take offence at anything that I say or do and I love you for that. It will take me a lifetime just to tell you how much you mean to me. Your eyes speak volumes. They have so much depth in them. In fact, I find everything admirable about you and thank God everyday for bringing you into my life. Sorry guys for holding up the party here. Coming to the point, Riya I wish to dedicate a song to you to let you know that I will need you till my last dying breath.'

The DJ played the track I had requested and I started singing the song along with the rest of the crowd.

Soniyo, O Soniyo, Tumhe dekhta hun toh sochta hun bas yahi,
Tu de de mera saath, tham le haath, chahe jo bhi baat,
Tu bas, de de mera saath.

'And all this while, I was thinking you were a bathroom singer. Those were some pretty decent vocals, Aditya. I must say I'm impressed,' said Riya.

'Ha! My voice is pathetic! Don't tell me I can sing well,' I replied.

'Shut up. I know you better than you do. So don't argue with me. If I say you're a good singer, then you are. No further discussions on it,' said Riya.

'Point taken, Madam,' I replied.

Once the song ended, everyone cheered for us and gave us a resounding applause.

Riya told me I was being particularly mushy that day and checked if I was fine.

Holding her hand in mine, I said, 'Riya, what is life without passion? The feeling of a shared experience—of waiting to be caressed, wanting to explode—like a wild sensation of fulfilment. When you look into my eyes, it is a feeling that I can't ignore. You give me all the reasons in the world to believe that you won't hurt me in anyway. If I ever lose you, I don't know what I would do. You probably think that I am crazy, but it's my love for you that makes me behave like one.'

With that, our day at the water park came to an end.

While returning home, I was once again preoccupied with thoughts of Mohit and Sonam. I told Riya about my wish to set them up together so that they could get an opportunity to come close.

'Even if Sonam did love Mohit, she won't speak her heart out. Mohit should instead take the initiative and speak to her.'

'Since Mohit doesn't have any other friends in Mumbai, the onus of setting them up lies on us too. I will talk to him tomorrow about this in office. You do the same with Sonam and we'll take it from there,' I said.

'Yes, that's a good idea.' Riya seemed quite excited about the whole thing.

We reached Riya's apartment. It had been a great weekend. Riya got down and gave me one last tight hug before retiring for the day.

Once home, I gave Mohit a call. He told me he had added Sonam on Facebook and that they had been incessantly chatting for the last two hours. I asked him if the conversation drifted towards their feelings for each other. But he told me he didn't want to risk his friendship with Sonam by expressing his feelings for her since he wasn't sure she would respond with equal zeal. I decided to have a long talk with Mohit tomorrow in the office.

Next morning, I called up Riya to remind her that she had to discuss things over with Sonam. I reached the office and went straight to Mohit's cabin, but he wasn't in. So I turned on my system and went to the cafeteria for a quick snack.

Mohit called me and said he would reach in ten minutes. I completed all my pending work and once Mohit arrived, we went to the smoking zone to talk.

I lit a cigarette and asked Mohit, 'Whatever you told me yesterday, was it true or were you kidding? I mean are you serious about her?'

'Of course I am. Why do you think I have been spending so much time with her since the past couple of days? I am trying to build a base here, my friend. You think I am faking it or that my intentions are bad? I could have a million girls queued up outside my house, but it is only Sonam that I have truly lost my heart to. I have fallen in love with her, goddammit!

I had never seen him like this before. He seemed totally smitten by Sonam!

'What kind of questions did you ask her? Does she have a boyfriend?' I asked curiously.

'No. She is single. Her last relationship was in college three years back. She told me that the reason she broke up with her boyfriend was owing to the fact that he was getting increasingly possessive about her and it was getting difficult for her to handle that. She says she has moved on in life and doesn't think too much about her failed relationship—I really admire her for that, Aadi. I admit I know very little about her, but I also know that if I were to get married one day, I'd want a life partner like Sonam,' said Mohit with an honesty that is hard to define.

'That says a lot, my boy. One date and you are thinking of marriage? Neat. You seem to know quite a lot about her. I just hope she likes you as much as you do,' I replied.

'I think she does. She seemed very eager to get acquainted with me and I can tell she was looking for excuses to call me up,' said Mohit.

'Dumbass, then why didn't you propose to her? You should have at least given her a hint that you like her. Do it before she finds someone else,' I said.

'I fear rejection, Aadi. You don't understand. I don't

want to lose her even as a friend. Only time will tell what course our friendship takes,' said Mohit with a tinge of sadness in his voice.

Soon after, I called Riya and told her about my conversation with Mohit. She told me she had spoken to Sonam who sort of gave her a hint that she too liked Mohit.

However, she is waiting for Mohit to take the first step,' said Riya.

'Let's meet today after our respective shifts are over. We'll chalk out a plan of action to bring them closer,' I told her.

I met Riya after the shift as decided. Sonam had left for home by the time I reached. Riya sat on my bike and we cruised comfortably on the road, discussing mission Mohit-Sonam.

'I think we should all meet after our shift tomorrow and go out somewhere. If they spend some more time together, sooner or later they are bound to express their feelings for each other. What do you think?' I asked Riya.

'Yes, that may work. Tomorrow, there is a wonderful play being staged in Navi Mumbai. My friend gave me for free passes of the same as she handles the stage equipment. She was highly recommending it. The play is a romantic drama and I've heard that it is definitely worth watching.'

'Great. I hope it works. However, let them sit separately from us and watch the act. That way, they can have a bit of privacy. Remember when we went to watch our first movie together? Even though the movie was horrible, we failed to notice it since we were so engrossed in each other,' I smiled.

'I remember very well. You were all over the place. I mean over me,' she winked.

'So tomorrow it is then,' said Riya.

When you fall in love, nothing can change the way you feel. Your heart starts beating like a train on a track. You fail to notice anything around you except for your loved one's face that keeps looming large over your head. Things like food and sleep become secondary. You don't even realize that you haven't eaten all day. You can't sleep thinking about them and when you are with them, you can barely speak. Mohit was going through the same ordeal. I don't remember him eating anything during lunch break. If his behaviour for the past two days is anything to go by, love is definitely in the air.

Hooked and Booked

We met outside the theatre in Navi Mumbai. The play was called *Love is a Losing Game*. Various posters had been put up on the bulletin board and walls of the theatre right upto the first floor where the play was going to be staged. We took our tickets and went inside. Once in, we saw that a few people were already seated, patiently waiting for the show to begin. It was a mixed crowd of people across all age groups. But it wasn't as crowded as I had expected it to be. Riya and I didn't speak much as we were busy observing Mohit and Sonam who had settled down on their seats two rows ahead of us. The seemed to be having a good time even before the play had started! Riya poked my arm and looked at me in disdain for peeping into their seats. We settled into our seats and the play commenced.

The narrator's voice boomed out describing the initial plot to the audience. The two lead characters—Aman and Ananya—had been close friends since school, but this friendship never culminated into anything more.

As the curtains drew open, the first scene enfolded. It was that of a class trip and showed the lead characters sitting together in a garden gazing into the sky. Ananya expresses her frustration and boredom to Aman, wishing she had a boyfriend with whom she could spend her time. Aman tells her that he feels the same way and thinks they are the only ones in their friend circle who are without a partner. Everbody else seems to have found their perfect 'other'. They decide to play a game in which both of them will date each other for eighty days to see if they are compatible enough to be together for the rest of their lives.

How ingenious, I thought to myself.

Then a stage boy passed by from one end of the stage to the other with a placard saying 'Day 1' to indicate the passage of time.

On their first date, both are shown standing outside a concert hall. Aman gifts Ananya a star-shaped keychain before the show begins. Their awkwardness is quite evident as it is their first date.

'I must say their acting is spot on,' I mumbled to Riya who nodded in agreement.

On Day 3, both are shown having a good time at a friend's birthday party which also marks the first time they hug one another.

On day 7, the characters are sitting together by the beach, watching the sun go down. As the evening turns into night the snuggled couple gaze at the canopy of stars above. Ananya spots a shooting star and closes her eyes to make a secret wish. Even on constant prodding to reveal what she had wished for, she keeps it to herself, saying to Aman that the divulgence of the wish would only reduce the chance of it coming true.

On day 18, they spend time at the annual city fair. Aman takes Ananya to the House of Horror where she grabs someone else's hand by mistake. When she realizes this, both break into laughter.

On day 50, they kiss for the first time after watching a movie. They pass by a fortune teller who advises them to treasure every moment from now on. Thinking it to be a madman's mumbo jumbo, both take it lightly and move ahead.

Day 65 is another day at the beach where they end up getting intimate in the company of the setting sun—a picture perfect moment.

On day 79, they decide to go on a picnic to the park. While basking in the sun, Ananya requests Aman to get her a bottle of apple juice. Aman says he will be back in no time and walks off to look for a street vendor, making a hurried exit from the stage. Time passes by but there is no sign of Aman, adding to Ananya's worries. She paces up and down the length of the stage, waiting for him to show up. Then she sees a man walking towards her. He asks her if her name is Ananya. Fearing the worst, she slowly nods her head in agreement. He tells her that he was walking down the street when out of nowhere came this big truck that mowed down a young guy who was crossing the road. He then tells Ananya that he went charging towards the boy who was lying in a pool of blood. That's when he heard the boy shout Ananya's name, making him come and look for her.

Ananya runs over to the spot with the stranger and sees Aman lying injured on the road. Ananya notices that he is still holding onto the juice with a shivering hand. Semi-conscious, he tries to hand over the drink to her. She can't hold back her tears any further and breaks into hysterical sobs. By that time, a sizeable crowd has gathered around them and one of them hurriedly calls for an ambulance. On reaching the hospital, Aman is carried straight to the emergency room. All Ananya can do at this point is sit outside and wait—for eight long hours.

The scene changes to a night later. At 11.40 pm, the doctor comes out of the emergency room and says, 'I am sorry but we did the best we could. His injuries are so grave that he only has a few minutes to live. Here, we found a letter in his pocket. You might want to take a look at it.'

The doctor hands over the letter to Ananya after which she goes into the room to see Aman. He looks weak, but peaceful. Ananya reads the letter and bursts into tears. The letter says:

Ananya,

Our eighty days are almost over and I must say I have spent my life's best moments with you. I don't know whether I will be able to tell you how much I love you after all this is over. Maybe that is why I am writing this letter in the first place. Now that I am nearing the end, I want to tell you that the game was a mere ploy to get you to spend time with me. The truth is I have been in love with you since school days but could not get myself to reveal my true feelings. I have and will always love you. I have nothing much to ask for, but just wish that I could extend our time together by another day. I want to be yours forever. I love you, Ananya, and I am sorry for not expressing my feelings before. Hope you will be mine, always.

Ananya holds Aman's hand and says, 'Do you know what I wished for the night I saw the shooting star? I asked God to never let our eighty days together come to an end. You can't leave me alone like this. I love you. Please come back to me. I really love you, Aman, and have done so since school days but never had the courage to express my feelings.'

As the clock strikes twelve, Aman's heart stops beating. His death marks the end of their eightieth day together.

With this the play came to an end after which the lead protagonists came and stood at the centre of the stage, took a bow to a rapturous applause, and graciously departed.

As I got up from my seat to head towards the exit, I noticed that there was not a single dry eye in the theatre. I heard a few ladies discussing the plot ending, wishing aloud how Aman should have expressed his feelings to Ananya while he was still alive. Their thoughts exactly echoed my own sentiments. *But then*

if one could predict the tragic end, one would refrain
from getting into that relationship in the first place,
I thought to myself.

Riya was right. This play was definitely worth
watching. The last hospital scene sent shivers down my
spine. We went outside the theatre where Mohit and
Sonam were patiently waiting for us. All four of agreed
that the play was really good. Sitting in the hall for two
hours had jammed our legs, so we decided to walk for
sometime. Mohit and Sonam were silently walking a
few steps ahead of us. It was ultimately Mohit who
broke the ice.

'Did you like the play?' Mohit asked.

'Yes, very much. It made me cry,' replied Sonam.

Their conversation ended here. Mohit took out his
cell phone from his pocket and started writing a text
message. Sonam heard her phone beep.

Taking out her mobile phone from her bag, she
asked, 'You sent me a message?'

'Just read it, please,' Mohit replied.

She read the message out aloud:

It's lucky to love someone,

It's your fortune to love the one who loves you,

But it's a miracle to love a person who can't love anyone
except you

Seeing the play's tragic end, I decided to propose to
you. I do not want to suffer like Aditya nor keep my
feelings to myself. I want to do this before it's too late. I
love you Sonam, ever since our double date with Aditya

*and Riya. If you love me too, just hold my hand and kiss
me on my cheek.*

Mohit was walking straight without looking
sideways—too afraid to look at Sonam in the eye.
Sonam didn't react for some time, which made Mohit
all the more anxious. I could tell that he was probably
rethinking his decision because he had spoken about his
feelings in front of all of us. Sonam was walking ahead of
him without giving any sort of reaction to the message.
Before he could say anything, Sonam held his hand and
planted a kiss on his cheek. Mohit was astounded for
a moment. He looked above and closed his eyes. Her
reaction had left him speechless.

He then opened his eyes and kissed Sonam, this
time on her lips. Sonam did not resist—their wild kiss
kept them so engrossed that they even failed to notice
us standing beside them.

'Never in my wildest dreams did I think that I
would meet someone in Mumbai and fall in love with
her instantly. I had left this decision to my parents
since I have faith in their choice. But I will have to
rethink my decision now, since I have fallen head over
heels in love with you, Sonam. I love you with all my
heart and now I know you too do,' said Mohit and
kissed her hand.

'And never did I think that I'll fall in love with
someone right after a casual first date! I never wanted
to be in another relationship after my first one turned

out to be a disaster. I don't know but there is something so special about you that I just can't help myself but be drawn to you. I love you too, Mohit,' said Sonam smiling.

Once they broke the long embrace, Riya went and hugged Sonam while I gave Mohit a pat on his back.

'Now all four of us can hang out together,' said Riya with excitement. We did not want to disturb them just yet, wanting to give their relationship some time to develop.

When Mohit reached office the next day, I had already logged in and was taking my regular calls. I told him to meet me during lunch break. The day had been hectic with back-to-back client calls for non-stop four hours. I did not have even a minute to spare. After my session got over, I took my first break and met Mohit. He looked visibly upset.

'What happened? Did you pick up a fight with Sonam?' I enquired.

'No. But you know, I officially proposed to her yesterday. She had accepted it, right? But later at night, she gave me a call saying this will not work out as she loves someone else,' Mohit replied.

'What the fuck! You had told me she was single and has moved on. Even Riya told me so. How is this possible?' I replied, stunned by what I was hearing. All along, I had been under the impression that Sonam loved him too. I had heard him say so many times and so had Riya. How could we have been so wrong about this?

Mohit just stood there with a glum expression.

I continued speaking, 'What did she say? Did she tell you she doesn't love you? Oh whatever, Mohit! Don't be upset. You are a smart guy and are financially stable, you can get any girl you want. Look at our new HR manager. Now that girl is hot! By the looks of her, I can tell you she will be wild in bed.'

'Aadi stop it, yaar. I am not in a mood to joke,' said Mohit in a sad tone.

'Hey, I'm serious. Why don't you give it a shot? Just turn around and look at her, will you?' I said pointing towards the girl who was handing out access cards to new employees.

'Forget it. It's useless trying to fool you—you end up taking everything so seriously, yaar. I was joking. All's good between Sonam and me,' said Mohit.

'You bastard! I will kill you. I really thought you were serious about it. So you've made a big fool out of me, haan?' I said.

Both of us looked at each other and burst out laughing.

'Okay, first things first. Go change your relationship status from "single" to "committed" on Facebook.

Finally, you mustered the courage to propose and waah beta, you even kissed her! Too fast, too close. Carry on. Sonam is a nice girl and I must say, you both look great together,' I told him.

Mohit smiled and thanked me for all the support. I was happy that I played a small part in setting up two people who seemed just right for each other. *Maybe I should open up a marriage bureau*, I thought to myself.

Once home, I called Riya and told her that Mohit and Sonam were officially in a relationship now. She was elated and told me she had known this from the first day of their date. We both were extremely happy and excited for them.

Sonam was a beautiful, young lady and Mohit a handsome, intelligent man with. They both looked perfect with each other. It made me think about how blessed I was to have Riya in my life.

Love comes through eyes, as they help me see you, Riya. Love comes through ears, as they help me hear your soft voice. Love comes through hands, as your touch sends shivers down my spine. Love comes through dreams, as I dream about the life you have imparted me. Love comes through smiles, as I fall for you every time you smile. Love comes through our tight embrace, making me feel secure in your arms. Love comes through the heart, as my heart skips a beat whenever I see you and love comes through me. Love comes through you, Riya, and through Sonam and Mohit. So this is what true love is all about.

Later in the day, when all four of us met outside our favourite hangout place, Mohit and Sonam decided to visit a temple and asked us if we wanted to join them. We instantly agreed and suggested we go to the famous Siddhivinayak temple situated in Dadar.

'I've heard that it is not considered a good omen for unmarried couples to visit the temple. What I mean to say is that couples should only visit that temple post marriage. Otherwise it is said to ruin their relationship,' said Mohit cautiously.

'Yes I have heard that too. Lord Ganesh curses those couples who visit him before marriage,' Sonam added.

Riya and I looked at each other, recalling the day we had taken the seven holy promises in secret a few months back without telling anyone.

'If you ask me, I personally don't believe in it. We had visited this very temple a few years back and look, we are still together. It's all rubbish if you ask me. Don't believe in all these things,' I said.

'I hope so. Fine, let's all go to the temple,' said

Sonam. Mohit still looked a bit doubtful about the whole thing.

'Look, if you don't go to the temple, does it give you any sort of guarantee that your future life will be smooth with Sonam? No one can predict these things. Why do we believe in things which are not practical? Things are bound to happen even if you try to stop them. You can't control everything in life,' I said trying to explain things to Mohit.

He finally gave in and we decided to visit the temple together. We went to our respective homes for a quick change of clothes. Since we were going to a religious place, traditional wear was what seemed like the practical choice. I was the first one to get dressed and picked up everyone in my car after which we headed off to Dadar.

Riya looked like a perfect wife in her traditional salwar kameez. I had hardly seen her in a traditional clothes since the nature of her job demanded she wear western wear. I personally always liked her more in traditional oufits, with minimal makeup on. Sonam and Mohit sat on the backseat, this time much closer to each other, with Sonam resting her head comfortably on his shoulders. We teased them along the journey. We loved the way they blushed during our leg-pulling session.

As Riya got of the car near the temple premises, she threw a quick glance at me. Inside her head, I knew she was thinking the same thing that had kept my mind occupied all through morning.

'Those were such innocent days, right?' I said trying to harp back on the old days.

'Yes. They were. I will always cherish the seven promises that we took in this temple,' said Riya affectionately. She pulled my cheeks and smiled.

I held Riya's hand and all four of us went inside the temple. It was Mohit and Sonam's first visit and they thanked us for bringing them there. We took the blessings of Lord Ganesh. I looked at Riya when we were praying. She had closed her eyes and with her hands clasped, she was muttering a silent prayer. I wanted to officially marry her at that moment itself. I looked at Mohit who was busy tickling Sonam while she was trying to pray. The pundit told them to behave. I closed my eyes and made a silent prayer to God:

Oh, God. You have given me everything. You gave me Riya back in my life. I don't expect anything more from you. I just pray to you to let Mohit and Sonam live happily ever after and not face the pain of separation like we did before. Thank you for whatever you have given me in life.

Once back in the car, Mohit asked us, 'Be serious now, guys. When are you planning to get married?'

Riya avoided answering the question and instead cleverly directed it towards me.

'Why don't you answer that, love?' she said.

'We will, Mohit. However, we still have to talk to our parents about this. Besides, I have already told you before that we are still too young for marriage. And I know that Riya has some goals that she wants to achieve before finally taking the plunge. So to answer your question, as of now we are not thinking about marriage. But who knows what the future holds?' I said, trying to explain the complicated dynamics of our relationship as best as I could.

'But jaan, does marriage really matter? I am proud to be your partner,' said Riya resting her head on my shoulders.

'Now let me ask you the same question. When is the D-day?" said Riya putting them in a spot again.

Mohit and Sonam remained quiet for a while.

'Sonam, I think you must rethink your decision to be with Mohit because he may turn out to be gay. Mohit, why don't you marry that Bandra guy who was chasing you the other day on the beach? He clearly seemed very interested in you. Plus, section 377 of the IPC now makes it legal,' I winked. Digging up old demons of the person asking you difficult questions is the best trick to shut them up.

'I will kill you one of these days, Aditya. If not me, either Riya or Sonam will. That's for sure,' said Mohit and we all broke into laughter.

Over time, we started enjoying each other's company. Even though Mohit was my team leader, he behaved more like an elder brother. Though we had become friends only recently, it strangely felt like I had known him since a long time. Since my other close friend Sameer was too preoccupied in preparing for his civil service exams, I didn't disturb him too much. I had found a nice friend in Mohit, and Riya was always with me for support. I believed Sonam was the perfect choice for Mohit. I wished all four of us would get married soon. I wished for a perfect ending to both our love stories.

Double Delight

'**O**rganizations spend the majority of their resources on finding external candidates and training them. However, the most cost effective and practical thing is to hire someone from within. Our company is doing the same. We have internal job postings (IJP) this week,' our manager told us during the weekly meeting.

I had applied for the IJP long back. For an IJP, managers from different branches would conduct an assessment followed by an interview with the senior-level management.

After the shift, I called up Riya and said excitedly, 'Jaan, we have IJP's in our office and I have applied for it. If I get through, then my salary will be approximately 30k per month.'

'That's great news. I too have IJP's in my department next week. I hope I get through. Mom will be happy if I get an increment. My gross salary will be around 40k.'

'Excellent. It means both of us will make about 70k

per month. That's not a bad figure. I am so happy for you. I know you will make it,' I said positively.

I wanted to get through for Riya's sake. She knew how hard I had worked for the past few years and prayed for me to clear my IJP.

A week later, the day of the assessment arrived.

I logged onto my system and saw that a test awaited me.

The questions were not difficult as they were process related which was my area of expertise. I had worked in the same process for months now and knew about it in and out. The given time limit was ninety minutes, but I finished the assessment in eighty minutes flat. Since I had time on hand, I rechecked all my options. An aggregate of 95 percent was required to clear the assessment. I submitted the answers and waited for the auto evaluation.

Employee Id: 094837 has cleared the assessment with 96 percent.

I was overjoyed even though I knew the outcome would be such. I called Riya and told her about the result. She couldn't stop congratulating me. I knew that the most difficult hurdle to cross was the interview. Nevertheless, I had moved one step closer to my dream.

One hour later, my interview began.

'Hello Aditya, How are you doing today?' asked one interviewer as soon as I took my seat in the conference room.

'Very well, sir; how are you?'

'I am good. So Aditya, how long have you been working for SGS?'

'It's been more than six months, sir. I have been working very hard to increase my net satisfaction score and I am proud of the fact that I was able to achieve most of the targets assigned to me,' I told him proudly.

'It's good to hear how devoted you are towards work. I hope your score will become even better with time. Your team leader has some really good things to say about you. He tells me that you have been consistently performing well ever since you joined the company,' said the interviewer.

I made a mental note to thank Mohit for putting in a good word for me.

'Thank you, sir. I will serve SGS with all my heart and vouch to improve with each passing day,' I promised.

He asked me several other questions and after an hour long interview, he thanked me for coming and I took his leave. I had no idea about how my interview had gone. *Did I seem too nervous? What if they don't like me?* A million unanswered questions were running through my head.

We were told that the results of the interview would be declared that day itself. This added to my nervousness. But in my heart, I could see myself securing the IJP. The figure of thirty thousand rupees loomed large over my eyes.

I called up Riya in the meantime. I told her how my interview had gone and she could tell how nervous I was. I told her that I wanted to secure the IJP for her, to make her happy. I wanted to see a smile on her face and happiness in her eyes.

'Don't worry, Aadi. I am always with you. Just close your eyes and think of me standing in front of you, holding you tight and making you feel like nothing can go wrong in your life. I know you will clear your IJP. Just chill,' she said and hung up.

I sat on the chair with my fingers crossed. The HR team appeared shortly to announce the results. Mohit was on the ground floor, supervising calls. I so wished he was by my side in this hour of difficulty. The HR manager started reading out names from the list. I jumped when my name was announced. I wanted to hug the girl and shout like a madman. I went hurriedly to the ground floor and told Mohit that I had cleared the interview. He gave me a high five and seemed genuinely happy for me.

Aditya
Senior Management Expert (SME)

My new designation sounded like music to the ears! I was thrilled. I called up Riya immediately and gave her the good news. I could feel she was on the verge of tears, as she knew the importance of appraisals and how difficult it was to secure an IJP. Now that I had made it through, she told me about her growing fears about the interview next week. I gave her a pep talk and told her not to worry too much. She hung up after congratulating me again for the millionth time that evening.

One week later, we were going through the same ordeal, but this time with Riya at the receiving end. Since work got over early that day, Mohit and I had gone to her office to boost her morale. Sonam had joined us too. Both Mohit and I were smoking while waiting for her interview to get over. Mohit told me I looked more nervous for Riya's interview than I did during my own. Earlier at the office, I had called her roughly ten times in an hour to know the updates. Now in her office, the incessant wait was getting too much for me to bear. Riya had been inside the interview cabin for more than an hour. I desperately wanted to know how things were proceeding, praying she'd make it through. It was not because I wanted her to earn more than me but because I knew how her family could do with a bit more money.

After an hour, Riya called me up to tell me that her assessment had gone well but she won't be able to come down to meet us as the HR person had asked her to wait for the results.

I continued smoking out of nervousness. Sonam shouted at me for my incessant smoking, scolding me as if I was a criminal. However, I ignored her. *This is not the right time to tell me not to smoke*, I wanted to say. Riya called me after five minutes.

'Aadi, I cleared the assessment with a 98 percent score,' said Riya over the phone.

I couldn't control my happiness and hugged both Mohit and Sonam. I was elated with the news. I knew that there is no stopping to Riya now and that she would definitely clear her interview too. Mohit and Sonam chatted while I went and bought some chips and cold drinks for us.

'What do you think, will Riya clear her interview?' I asked Sonam while handing her the soft drink she had asked me to get for.

'I have no doubts about it. Plus, she has loads of experience, which is more than enough for the post of a team leader. Her performance too has been excellent over the past few months. There is no reason why she shouldn't be promoted,' replied Sonam.

Hearing this, I calmed down a little. There was no way they would not promote her. She called me up after about twenty minutes saying her interview was over and that it had gone very well. She told me that the results would be out within an hour. Sonam went upstairs to give her company. Mohit told me to wait with him for a few minutes.

As soon as Sonam headed upstairs, Mohit took out a cigarette and started smoking. Since Sonam did not like people who smoked, Mohit would do it on the sly.

'Have you been smoking since college or did work pressure get to you and you ended up smoking on the job?' I asked Mohit.

'I started smoking during the first year of college. Everyone else seemed to be doing it, so I too gave it a try. It became a habit ever since. But I wouldn't call myself a heavy smoker. Just one or two smokes a day is sufficient for me. I know what hazardous effect it can have on my body and I don't want that to happen since my family's responsibility lies on my head,' said Mohit.

I could see the sense in his argument. But even though I agreed with what he had to say, I knew I could not implement it in my own life. Smoking had become a staple for me.

'Sounds interesting. So will you quit smoking after marrying Sonam?' I asked.

'Yes. I will. She knows I smoke, but I have promised her that I will quit smoking after marriage.'

Just then, Mohit's cell phone beeped. It was a message from Sonam. He read it out aloud.

Riya has cleared the interview. We have been trying to call you guys, but your phone is unreachable. Why don't both of you join us upstairs?

Mohit and I ran to the first floor. Riya was standing in the lobby with Sonam. I gave her a tight hug and lifted her off her feet. When I finally put her down, she leaned towards me and gave me a kiss on my forehead. I wanted to scream and tell her how much I loved her. It was difficult for me to control my emotions. I knew this appraisal meant a lot to Riya and her family.

True love is a sacred flame that burns eternally. Today's hug was so special that it can't be expressed in words. I held her tightly for a long time. I wiped her tears and hugged her again.

Waqt har cheez dikhaata hai
Aaj samajh aaya hai.
Kitne barso baad
Aaj fir tujhpe marne ka khayaal aaya hai.
Chal kahin door chale, jahan sirf tu or main ho
Jee le apne zindagi ke wo haseen pal jisme sirf pyaar ho.
Baahon me baahein ho, aankhon me aankhein ho
Bas tumhara khayaal ho, aur sirf tumhara saath ho.

Three months later…

'Listen up Aadi. I am bored with our daily routine and desperately need a change,' said Mohit while we were having food in the cafeteria. Both Riya and Sonam had left for their respective homes.

'Let's plan a trip. We will go somewhere far off for two weeks. We must apply for a leave now,' I suggested.

'That's a great idea. Sonam too wanted to go visit her parents,' said Mohit in excitement.

'Really? How about going to Delhi and Manali?'

'Oh! I hope Sonam agrees to go. Let me ask her once I reach home,' said Mohit.

'Yes you do that. In the meanwhile, I will try and persuade Riya to come along too. Getting permission from her parents would be a bit difficult, so we will have to think of a good excuse to convince them. Oh, it will be so much fun,' I said smiling.

Mohit called me up later that night to tell me that Sonam had agreed to come on the trip. She believed it would be a good relief from the monotony of going to office everyday and doing the same mechanical work over and over again. She also suggested that while in Delhi, we could stay at her guest house which is quite near her house in South Delhi. She also liked the proposed of going to Manali. Mohit then asked me if Riya had agreed too and I told him that I had been on the phone with her precisely a minute before his call and that she was equally excited. We decided to call this an office trip so as to convince our parents.

It was Monday evening. I was having dinner with my Mom. I could sense that she was in a good mood.

'Mom, this coming weekend my company is planning to send me on an official work trip to Delhi for few days,' I lied.

'Are you sure? I hope you have not planned a trip with your friends,' my mother questioned sounding suspicious.

'Why would you think that? You can ask my team leader. He too is coming along with me,' I said, having already forewarned Mohit that my Mom could give him a call to enquire.

To my surprise, Mom instantly agreed and asked me the number of days the trip would last.

'The trip is for eight days but I am not sure whether it would be extended it or not. The team is leaving for Delhi on Friday night. Our company is taking care of the accommodation but all other expenses have to be individually borne by us.'

Mom asked me a few more questions regarding the trip and I was finally able to convince her to let me go. I went into my room and messaged Riya.

My sweetheart, I told my Mom about the Delhi trip and she has agreed to let me go. She did have a few reservations about it as she could sense I was lying. However, I managed to convince her. I told her that the company was paying for our accommodation. So gear up, Madam—I am all set to love you. Two weeks without parents—just you, me, Mohit, and Sonam.

She replied back saying she was yet to tell her mother about the trip and would do so after dinner. Meanwhile

I sent a message each to Sonam and Mohit telling them that my parents had agreed. We were just waiting for Riya to confirm after which we could apply for leaves. Everyone kept their fingers crossed.

The next day, Riya recounted the exact conversation she had with her Mom the previous night. She told us that after I had hung up the phone, she had an early dinner and called her Mom to her room to resolve an urgent matter. Her Mom asked her if she was facing any problem at work.

She had told her Mom that it was an official trip organized by the company and that the entire team had to go for it since they had been asked to meet high-end clients in Delhi with whom they had maximum interaction. She further told her mother that she had to leave for Delhi on Friday evening for an eight-day trip.

Her Mom had questioned her about the expenses to which Riya had told her that the company would pay for their accommodation and railway tickets.

Riya told us how her mother was still not convinced, saying that the trip would turn out to be a costly affair and reminding her of the critical financial condition of their family. She said that Riya should have denied the offer when it came to her!

'I made it clear to her that it's not like I get to choose these things. The management board had asked our team to go and we had to agree to their decision and that I don't have a say in it. She dismissed me by saying that she will confirm after talking to my Dad in the morning,' recounted Riya.

All three of us were tuned in to her woes.

'My mother's cold response makes me feel that she would not agree to let me go on the trip. I cried all through the night. She thought that because of her the entire plan would fizzle out and none of us would be able to go. I tried my best to convince her.'

'Jaan, we all understand your situation and even if your Mom doesn't agree to let you go, its okay. You can try convincing her again one last time tomorrow,' I said, trying my best to console her.

The next day while I was getting ready for work, I got a message from Riya:

Mom has agreed to let me go. I am so glad that I can barely believe it. I cannot wait to meet you and see the happiness on your face. You are the best boyfriend in the world. I will never let go of someone so precious to me. I love you. I want to live these eight days with you without a single worrying thought. The world seems to be a totally different place with you by my side. It's like a beautiful, never-ending dream. I promise to love you forever. You are my Mr Perfect.

I messaged Riya back saying:

My imagination is full of dreams—both happy and sweet ones. You are a flower in full bloom; your radiant smile brightens up my day. If I tried to paint you, no colours would be able to describe your true beauty. And yes, I am eagerly looking forward to our passionate nights in Manali. Love you a lot. Muaahhh!☺

Since all four of us had been pretty regular to office, we had a lot of pending leaves. So securing leave from office was a piece of cake for us. We went holiday shopping to Bandra and Malad. Since we were also going to Manali, as a precaution we took a few woollen clothes in case the weather got cold. For the Delhi heat, we took a few summer outfits as well. I couldn't wait to see how short and revealing Riya's clothes were.

Everyone was pretty excited about the trip but Sonam and Mohit looked more excited than us since it was their first trip together. Thankfully, we had informed our parents that if need be the trip could extend by a few days. We got our tickets booked for Friday night, Garib Rath AC. It was a sixteen-hour journey to New Delhi and we had decided to stay at Sonam's guest house. I could not wait to spend a few passionate moments with Riya alone in our room.

I thought about what we would do on our first night together. *First, I could dim the lights and carry her to the bed. We could then start with a passionate kiss on the lips followed by smaller kisses all over her body.* I could imagine our bodies melting together as one.

I pushed aside these thoughts from my mind and headed for the railway station.

Jab they Met her Parents

We boarded the train and took our seats. A group of young boys and girls were sitting next to us. I kept our luggage under the berth and settled down on my seat. Riya sat beside me while Mohit and Sonam had berths opposite ours. Even though Riya had come in casuals, she looked gorgeous. She was wearing brown capri parts and a loose white t-shirt with a sling bag looped around her shoulder. I looked outside the window where people were waving goodbye to their relatives. The train left Mumbai exactly on time.

A cool breeze blew through the open window which lifted a few strands of Riya's hair and brought them to her face. I slowly pushed them behind her neck and gently ran my fingers through her hair. After an hour or so, we decided to play antakshari. We also asked the other group to join us. They agreed and we made two teams. They were in one team and the four of us were in the other. They sung the first song which ended with the alphabet 'p'.

I started singing, 'Pyaar diwaana hota hai, mastaana hota hai. Har khushi se har gham se begaana hota hai…'

I was looking at Riya all the while and she kept blushing. It was their turn now.

Har ghadi badal rahi hai roop zindagi, chaav hai kabhi kabhi hai dhoop zindagi... Har pal yahan jee bhar jiyo, jo hai samar, kal ho na ho. 'Its "h" for you,' said a guy in the other team.

Humein tumse pyaar kitna, ye hum nahin jaante, magar jee nahi sakte, tumhaare bina... Mohit held Sonam close to him while singing.

The songs continued for a while after which the ticket checker (TC) came and told us to either switch off the lights and go to off sleep or maintain silence for the sake of the other passengers on the train. All of us apologized for creating such a racket and retired to our respective berths. Riya sat with me on my berth for a bit longer. She kept her head on my chest and in the spur of the moment said, 'Let's get married'.

'You are anyway my wife. We just need to officially tie the knot. And that we will do soon,' I said kissing her on her forehead.

She went to her berth after sometime. Sonam too was fast asleep. Mohit and I were still awake, gossiping about girls. I took a packet of cigarettes from my bag and went towards the passage. Mohit followed me along with some of the other boys from the group. We stood near the door and checked if anyone was awake. The entire compartment seemed to be deep in sleep.

I lit a cigarette even though I knew smoking was prohibited in the train. However, I thought to myself that if the TC could drink alcohol on the sly, we could smoke too could. We bribed the TC to let us smoke. As I guessed, the lure of money was enough for him to temporarily forget his duties.

'Where are you from,' I asked the guys from the other group. They had followed us into the passage and were smoking along side.

'We are from Churchgate and are on our way to Agra,' said one of the boys.

'Is the Taj Mahal visible from the train?' asked Mohit.

'Yes, you can see it, but not during the night,' the same guy quipped.

We didn't know whether to take them at face value or not. They seemed like an innocent lot. We ended up gossiping on various topics late into the night. They asked us if the two girls accompanying us were our girlfriends. Their queries about the girls made me feel jealous and a bit possessive too. I felt like they had no right asking about them.

Gradually, our passage was filled with smoke, the smell of which woke up a few passengers. Before one of them could get a chance to get up and complain, we stopped smoking and went to our seats to retire for the night. Riya and Sonam were busy sleeping. I was excited because within fifteen minutes our train was going to stop at Ratlam station.

I shook Riya from her sleep, telling her that Ratlam was about to come. She was a big Kareena Kapoor fan and had seen the movie *Jab We Met* at least ten times. The train finally came to a halt at Ratlam station. We got down to see if it was similar to the movie. It did look like the station from the movie, except that it was a lot more crowded now. We disembarked and went to the nearest food stall. We asked for a water bottle and to our surprise, the vendor handed us a bottle with the label 'Jab We Met mineral water' written on it.

As I expected, Riya drank a sip of the water and said a dialogue from the movie in full filmy style, 'Paani ka kaam toh paani karta hai', leaving us laughing. We clicked a lot of pictures in different poses around the station. We asked the stall owner about Hotel Decent and whether such a place actually existed. He told us that there was in fact a hotel by that name which was at a fifteen minute dostamce from the station. I couldn't believe it and thought he was lying. A few moments later, we boarded the train and left.

Mohit and I played games on my laptop. We even browsed some tourism sites on the internet and particularly searched for honeymoon resorts in Manali. We wanted to make our partners feel special. We searched for a few and then went off to sleep.

We got up late in the morning. When we had already passed the Mathura station. New Delhi was still around two hours away. We freshened up and ordered a light breakfast from the train pantry. By the time Mohit and I returned from the washroom, Riya and Sonam had already eaten their share.

'What speed!' I teased the girls. They were sitting huddled up together in their blanket as the temperature had unexpectedly dropped that morning.

'Sonam, how far is your guest house from New Delhi?' I asked.

'It is pretty far from New Delhi station. But it will be easier for us if we get down at Hazrat Nizamuddin railway station instead as that is much closer to the guest house. We can hire a prepaid taxi from there. It should not take us more than an hour to reach,' Sonam replied.

Whenever a cold breeze passed us by, I used it as an excuse to hold Riya tightly.

At last after sixteen hours of journey, we reached the Hazrat Nizamuddin station. We got down from the train and crossed the bridge to hire a prepaid taxi. Mohit got into a brief argument with Sonam as she caught him smoking soon after disembarking the train. Both Riya and I laughed at them as they really didn't know how to quarrel.

It was an awesome feeling to be in the capital of India. Driving through the crowded streets of Delhi in cold winter is almost a novelty for most Mumbaikars since Mumbai weather remains almost the same throughout the year. The temperature in Delhi seemed to be below 10 degrees.

We were going to stay in Chittaranjan Park, which is popularly called CR Park by the locals. Sonam told us that it is a Bengali colony and is a peaceful area. It was nine kilometres away from the railway station. Our guest house was in 'B' block. While driving through Nehru Place, we also noticed the metro station.

'It's the violet line. Like in Mumbai we have the Western, Central, and Harbour lines for the local train, similarly, we have violet, red, and blue lines for the Delhi metro. With a major expansion plan underway, other lines are increasingly being added to the Metro, connecting all parts of Delhi with each other,' Sonam said pointing towards the metro station.

We were extremely excited with the prospect of exploring the city. I loved the big streets and the state embassies. Most of all, I loved how green Delhi was as compared to Mumbai. Rows of trees planted on either side of the road.

After an hour-long drive, we reached CR Park's B-Block. We took out our luggage and unlocked the gate of the guest house. The security guard was comfortably sleeping on the chair. Hearing the creaking sound of the gate, he suddenly woke up with a jolt.

Recognizing Sonam, he saluted us and helped open the gate. Sonam took the keys from him and we all walked along the passage. There was a black

Jeep parked outside the guest house. Sonam told us that it was her brother's prized possession. We went upstairs and lounged on the bed. Riya and I settled for the room which had a garden view. Sonam and Mohit kept their luggage in the other room. Our room even had a huge balcony and a king-size bed. A single beam of light entered the room through the gap between the curtains.

While Riya got busy unpacking, I went to check out the other room. Both rooms had been painted in different tropical colours. The theme running through them seemed Caribbean, with tropical plants placed in each corner of the room. I looked for Sonam who was in the kitchen making coffee for all of us. After the coffee, we went straight to our beds and slept for sometime so as to wear off the tiredness of the journey.

In the evening, Mohit and I went for a walk near Nehru Place metro station. Even though we noticed quite a few hot chicks cross our paths along the way, we didn't bother much about them as we had two equally hot girls with us at the guest house.

We made a spontaneous decision and decided to travel in the Metro. It was a completely new experience for us as the only one among us who had ever travelled by the metro was Sonam. We purchased tokens that enabled us to get on the train. We saw others using a card for easy entry and enquired if we could get one too instead of the tokens. It would have saved us much time while in Delhi because we would not have to stand in the queue to buy tokens every time we got on the metro.

The person at the enquiry counter was very helpful and provided us with a tourist card worth hundred rupees each, fifty out of which was refundable. I was concerned that we may not be able to use the full amount of the card and that it may not prove to be useful for occasional visitors like us, but the person at the counter told us that we would get the remaining balance whenever we returned the card.

I was impressed. After travelling in Mumbai local trains all my life, I found the Delhi Metro sophisticated, well connected, and one provided with a great serving staff. The crowning glory was of course its air-conditioned coaches to take care of the Delhi summer heat.

The girls joined us shortly on our metro ride through the city and we decided to head off to Lajpat Nagar. We were not allowed to click photographs once inside the Metro premises but still we managed to click a few on the sly. We reached Lajpat Nagar quite comfortably.

'Lajpat Nagar is a commercial joint, most famous for its kurtis and Indian wear. It is also one of the most crowded markets in Delhi,' Sonam explained.

'She is our tourist guide from today,' I teased her.

We shopped in Lajpat Nagar for an hour. Riya and Sonam purchased a few kurtis while Mohit and I accompanied them.

We reached our guest house in the evening and had an early dinner.

We then went to our respective rooms as the shopping expedition had tired us out and we knew a long day awaited us.

After changing into her nightwear, Riya dived straight into bed. She had coupled her tiny shorts with a grey crop top that left little to the imagination. I came and sat next to her, resting her head on my thighs.

'How was your first day in Delhi?' I asked her, gently stroking her hair.

'I love Delhi. Being here and visiting a few places made me get rid of a lot of misconceptions I had about the city. So many of my friends had warned me saying Delhi is not a safe place to be out alone in the night, especially for young girls. But personally speaking, I really like Delhi and would love to live here, if given an opportunity,' she replied while she stroked the palm of my hand with her fingers. Exactly my thoughts, I realized.

Since our room shared a common wall with Mohit and Sonam's room, we could easily hear whispers if listening carefully. At that precise moment, we had no difficulty in figuring out what they were upto.

'Now that's what I call "having a good time",' I teased Riya.

'Shut up Aadi. You are such a dog,' she laughed.

Riya and I shared the same blanket and got intimate, taking inspiration from our dear friends. After a passionate lovemaking session, we dozed off to sleep.

I woke up to a delicious feeling of warmth. The early morning sun was up before me. I let my eyes remain shut, allowing the rays to fall on them. I could feel two hands crawl their way towards my waist and knew Riya was up from her sleep. Then Riya got up and pulled open the curtains to let in the light. She walked towards the tray kept on the table and made me a nice cup of hot tea after which both of us stood in the balcony for some time.

The garden in front of the guest house was not clearly visible due to the heavy fog that engulfed the city. It was a sight to behold, one which I never saw in Mumbai. People were jogging in the garden—some by themselves, some with their spouses, and some with their pets for company. I sipped the tea looking at the row of houses in front of us. Mohit and Sonam were still sleeping. After their late night lovemaking session, they might have ended up sleeping late. Riya was still in same clothes that she wore last night. The sun rays made her skin glow.

We went inside. Mohit and Sonam were awake and discussing something on the dining table. We joined them in the conversation. I saw that both of them were looking serious. We all looked at another, waiting for someone to break the ice.

'Sonam is going to tell her parents that she loves me and wants to get engaged to me,' said Mohit.

'What the fuck! Are you serious? Oh my God! I can't believe it,' I shouted at the top of my lungs.

'That's amazing,' said Riya hugging Sonam

'That's amazing? Are you mad? That is way better than amazing! That's mighty awesome! I am so happy for you guys,' I shouted again.

Mohit was stunned to see our reaction. Maybe he didn't expect it coming. We all made him understand that we knew they would ultimately end up marrying but did not think it would happen so soon. Both Riya and I told them to go ahead with their decision. All four of us came together for a group hug after which we went to our respective rooms to get dressed. We wanted to wear something sophisticated as we were going to meet Sonam's parents.

Mohit wore a crisp white shirt with black jeans. He looked smart and was clearly dressed to impress. Both the girls took special care and wore traditional outfits, thinking that would help form the right impression in front of Sonam's parents. Once dressed, we took the Metro to her parent's house which was located near

AIIMS hospital in South Delhi. We boarded the Metro from Nehru Place and changed the metro line from Central Secretariat to take the line headed towards Huda City Centre, our stop being AIIMS.

I could see Mohit was getting increasingly nervous as we reached the apartment.

'Mohit, will you please relax? They won't kill you. Sonam has already given a hint to her parents about you. Moreover, her parents are not orthodox or narrow minded. She has told them that you live in Ahmedabad are work in Mumbai,' I said patting his back.

He tried to remain cool but the cold sweat on his brow spoke about his nervousness. Riya kept teasing him until we rang the bell and entered with house. A beautiful looking, middle-aged lady clad in a saree opened the door for us. I presumed she was Sonam's Mom from the way she ran up to her daughter and hugged her. Their house was huge and very well furnished. They seemed quite affluent. We sat on the sofa in the living room.

Soon Sonam's Mom emerged from the kitchen with glasses of juice on a tray which she coaxed us to take. Sonam introduced all of us one by one to her Mom. We exchanged greetings and she went into the kitchen to supervise the household chores and prepare something for us to eat.

My eyes kept searching for Sonam's Dad but I couldn't spot him anywhere. So I asked Sonam where he was.

'He is upstairs getting ready to go for work. He has asked us to make ourselves comfortable and that he will come down in sometime.' I am sure Sonam's words must have increased Mohit's heartbeats. I had never experienced such a situation except when I was drunk and had to leave Riya home. I always feared getting caught by her father and getting criticized for my act of insensitivity.

Her Mom came with pakoras in a plate.

'Is her Dad strict?' I whispered in Riya's ears. She just gave me a stern look. 'I simply asked because if he is, Mohit is screwed today,' I giggled.

'Beta, please eat some. I have made these especially for you. They are Sonam's favourite,' said Sonam's Mom handing me a plate of steaming hot pakoras. She came and sat on the chair next to the sofa.

'Aunty, it's lovely. I wish I could get such yummy homemade pakoras in Mumbai,' said Riya.

'You can come here anytime you feel like eating them. You don't get such pakoras in Mumbai?' asked her Mom.

'No. We don't. But the awesome chaat in Mumbai makes up for it,' said Mohit.

'I know. We call them golgappas. You should try the chole bhature in Delhi. You all will love it,' Sonam's Mom suggested.

I was about to say something when her Dad came downstairs. He had a grey mop of neatly combed hair. He was wearing a Lacoste t-shirt with denim jeans. He seemed pretty down to earth, nothing like the Hitler I had imagined him to be. He welcomed all of us and hugged Sonam. He glanced at Mohit as if sizing him up to see if the boy was worth his daughter.

'So are you guys enjoying Delhi?' he asked us.

We all nodded in agreement.

'Did you visit India gate?' It has become quite popular with youngsters after making an appearance in some Bollywood movies,' her Dad said making himself comfortable on the sofa.

'We have decided to go there tomorrow. We were too tired yesterday,' said Mohit, mustering some courage to speak in front of his 'probable' father-in-law.

Mohit then faced some basic rapid-fire questions that Indian families ask before giving their daughter away in marriage.

'I know today's generation does not like their parents to select a partner for them. They are too independent to care about such trivialities. I believe that times are changing and we as elders should adapt accordingly. So in short, we are open to the thought of you asking for our daughter's hand in marriage. If Sonam is happy with you, then we won't mind having you as our son-in-law,' her father said.

Sonam hugged her father tightly after which he got up and patted Mohit's back.

'I know that I am too young to say this in front of you, sir, but I will always try and keep Sonam happy to the best of my ability. We love each other and I am glad to have finally met you. I admit I was a little nervous at first, but you and Aunty have made me feel very comfortable and have welcomed me with open arms into your family. I am lucky to have a father-in-law like you,' said Mohit.

I smirked at how well he was sugar-coating the father.

Her Dad shook Mohit's hands and had a brief conversation with him in one corner. From his mannerisms, he seemed like a thorough gentleman. Meanwhile, we sat at the dining table and ate the lunch that Aunty had painstakingly prepared for us. We decided to leave without Sonam as she wanted to spend a little more time with her family.

Mohit took the blessings of her parents after which Riya and I touched his feet. Our actions made him realize we were a couple and he blessed us saying may we have a happy future together. I was amazed at how accurate his guess was. I realized that it is not easy hiding such stuff from elders. They have this innate ability to see through all our lies.

We reached our guest house by the metro. We brought a bottle of Champagne to celebrate. Riya didn't drink but she did not stop us either, as the cause for the celebration was huge. Sonam was almost engaged to Mohit!

By the time we finished our drinks, Sonam arrived and went straight to hug Mohit after which both kissed each other passionately in front of us.

'Sonam gets engaged to Mohit. Hip Hip Hurray!' we shouted.

I was so happy for them. They loved each other passionately. Two lives were soon going to embark on a new journey. I hoped that their engagement date got fixed soon and their love could have a fairy-tale start. I looked at Riya and saw that she had tears in her eyes. I knew what it meant. I kissed her tears away and told her I can't wait to share the same happiness with her.

'Let's go to Connaught Place for dinner. It is so lively in the evening,' said Sonam.

'Okay. Let's freshen up and move,' said Riya.

We left our guest house and reached the Nehru Place Metro station. From there, we boarded the train going to Rajiv Chowk, with a change of line at Central Secretariat. CP was crowded as we had expected, with a mix of corporate folks and youngsters. The place reminded me of Hiranandani Gardens in Mumbai. It was a lively place with many restaurants and food chains.

We went walking to Palika Bazaar first. It was an underground market with numerous cafes and eateries. The whole market was fully air-conditioned. We entered from Gate no. 1, which was the main gate to the market. It had a wonderful garden above, which made the place look even more beautiful. Couples were seen enjoying themselves in the garden.

We did not purchase anything much, just did a bit of window shopping. There were around four hundred shops closely huddled together in the underground market. We could not help but occasionally glance at the beautiful girls who were shopping there. No wonder Sonam and Riya kept giving us an 'I-will-kill-you' look. But deep down they knew it was all done in good jest. Sometimes, especially when you are in a different city, boys should be allowed to have a liitle bit of fun.

After that we went to the Dilli Darbar restaurant for dinner. The ambience of the restaurant was unlike any other restaurant we had been to before. Since happy hours got over by 7 pm, we didn't call for drinks as we had come in after that. For the main course, we opted for kadhai chicken with tandoori roti—a recommendation by Sonam who had visited the place before. She wasn't wrong either. It was simply delicious.

'I am in love with Delhi. If I get a chance to settle in Delhi, I won't think twice,' I said while going for a second helping of the chicken.

Riya took the serving spoon from my hand and kept it on the table. 'I know why you want to live in Delhi. So that you can gorge on kadhai chicken and add to your already expanding waistline,' she chided.

'No. I am serious. Mumbai people have so many misconceptions about Delhi. But being here, I can safely say that Delhi is really a pleasant city with nice people.'

We finished our dinner and left the place. It was getting increasingly cold. We reached our guest house and headed towards our bedrooms. Sonam and Mohit closed the door of their room. Riya and I cuddled togehter to keep ourselves warm. She dozed off in no time. I kept staring at her eyes and lips, kissing both gently. Soon I fell asleep. It had been two days since our arrival in Delhi and we loved every moment of it.

Earlier I believed that love was only a fable. Then quietly Riya came into my life and turned it into a reality. Our Delhi trip was turning out to be one hell of a dream.

The following day, we got up early as we had decided to go sightseeing around Delhi's famous spots. Sonam had taken permission to use her elder brother's jeep from her parents. Since he was currently out of town, Mohit agreed to drive the jeep around Delhi.

We left our guest house early feeling the chill of the morning breeze. Mumbaikars find it difficult to get accustomed to Delhi's winter. We had dressed sensibly for the weather in woollen jackets and scarves. The journey in the open jeep added to the thrill.

As we drove around Delhi streets from outer Ring Road to August Kranti Marg, we felt ourselves braving the winter winds. I could see the imposing structure of Qutub Minar from faraway. After parking our vehicle near the monument, we bought the entry ticket and entered the Qutab complex through the magnificent Alai Darwaza. I was fascinated with its architectural design. The heritage structure is said to be the tallest brick minaret in the world. The complex also housed a madarsa (school), graves, and mosques on either side of the gateway. The building made me think of ancient times when the Mughals would live here. The garden added to the beauty of the place. We clicked hundreds of photographs. I got attracted to the 'wish granting' iron pole in the courtyard of the Qutub minar. It was fenced with iron bars.

'It is believed that if you can encircle the pillar with hands behind your back and ask for a wish, your wish is bound to be fulfilled,' said Sonam.

'This is amazing. I wish it was not fenced. I would have wished for something for sure,' I said. 'The garden is the best part of this place. It's looking beautiful in the early morning fog.'

'Don't forget foreigners,' Mohit added as we sat on the rocks in the courtyard of Qutub.

'I don't like foreigners much. Have you seen how they come in the shabbiest clothes to India, like our country doesn't deserve any better?' I said.

We spent some time enjoying in the garden, clicked a few photographs around the area, and admired the overall beauty of the place.

Then we headed from August Kranti Marg towards Mahatma Gandhi Marg on our way to the Humayun

Tomb. Driving on Delhi streets in an open jeep was overall a thrilling experience. It took us a little less than half an hour to reach the spot. We parked our car and bought the entry tickets. It was a huge tomb set in a beautiful, peaceful garden, which I simply loved to the extreme. It was constructed of red sandstone and marble. As we walked in, we saw a notice board outside the gate with the name 'Char Bagh Garden' which had a huge fountain in the centre. This added to the beauty of the tomb.

'Sonam, was Taj Mahal built first or was it the Humayun tomb?' I asked.

'Humayun was Akbar's father, you idiot. Go and take some history lessons,' she shouted at me.

'Oh. I am sorry. I am weak in history,' I said smiling while the others laughed at me.

'Don't worry; I belong to your category. My knowledge of Indian history sucks too,' Mohit laughed. Sonam looked at him angrily but Mohit hugged her and kissed her forehead.

Sonam took us to the spot where the *Kurbaan* Movie song—Shukran Allah—was shot and the garden where they both sat together. Riya and I clicked some snaps of the place, sitting in a pose similar to Saif and Kareena with our arms around each other. We moved upstairs towards the tomb. The regal looking grave was surrounded by rooms. The grave of Emperor Humayun was located in the central room of the tomb. When we came outside, we saw many parrots flying around the white marbled dome of the tomb.

'It is said that these parrots are reincarnations of those people who couldn't complete their wishes before dying,' said Sonam smiling.

I didn't know whether she really believed it or not. I didn't dare ask her again as I was afraid she would narrate one of her many haunted stories. Before leaving, I turned back to look at the tomb once again so that its beautiful image stayed with me.

Next we drove from Mathura road to Chawri Bazaar next and reached our destination within an hour. Riya slept for some time in the jeep, keeping her head on my shoulders. Everyone was hungry and wanted something to eat.

As soon as we entered the Chandni Chowk area, I felt as if I had been ushered into a different city or a different world altogether. It was extremely crowded, and to make matters worse, the lanes were pretty narrow.

We went to eat paranthas at the famous 'Gali paranthe wali'. The first shop was Pandit Devi Daval's. All the shops had photographs of luminaries like Nehru, Indira Gandhi, and even Ranbir Kapoor dining at the shop. We tried rabdi parantha and badaam parantha, both made in pure ghee. Mohit and I managed to gobble down two each, but the girls could not eat beyond one since they found the paranthas too oily. We walked on the streets and saw another famous shop—'Jalebi waala'. Although our stomach was full beyond capacity, we could not resist sampling a few.

'You better not put on weight,' Riya shouted at me.

I loved how she scolded me for my eating habits. It only reaffirmed my belief on how much she cared about me. I was a big lover of junk food while she hated it. I forced her to take a bite of my jalebis and she surprisingly liked it.

We then decided to go to Jama Masjid but Mohit wanted to eat more. This time we decided to try Kareem's Restaurant. Once seated, we called for chicken biryani. The service was good but I didn't like the food at all. I felt we should have ordered for a curry item or something else with plain rice instead. Biryani was a bad choice. It was not as spicy as I had expected it to be and did not look well prepared.

To overcome the bad taste of the biryani, we made our way to 'The Ghantewala Halwai'.

'The trip to Chandni Chowk wouldn't have been complete if we had missed this one,' I said to Riya.

'So true. I love this Halwa. It's delicious,' she said eating a spoonful of the sohan halwa we ordered at the halwai shop.

All of us stood gazing at the shop's interiors. It looked ancient. I asked Sonam if she knew how old it was.

'It is one of the oldest sweet shops, not just in

Chandni Chowk but in the whole country, having served Mughal emperors and present-day politicians alike. I don't know precisely how old, but I can tell you that the present owner is a seventh generation guy,' she said. We were shocked at the good condition it was in.

Sonam then told us how the shop got its unusual name. In the Mughal days, the shop had a school located next to it where the bell would go off at regular intervals. And the great Mughal emperor Bahadur Shah Zafar, who was residing in Red Fort at that time, would call for sweets from the 'ghante ke neeche' shop.

'Incredible!' exclaimed Mohit.

I had heard many people call Chandni Chowk a down market and tacky place. However, I loved the experience of trying different dishes and felt that it was definitely an experience worth remembering.

It was late evening and the sun was about to set when we decided to head towards India Gate and Rajpath.

Before this, I had seen Rajpath only on news channels covering the Republic Day parade there every year. It was one hell of an experience driving an open jeep on that road. Not even for a second did I feel that I was in India. It was well maintained and well constructed.

As we drove near India Gate, we all stood up in the jeep and gave a warm salute to the Indian soldiers who sacrificed their lives for the country—taking the movie *Rang De Basanti* as our inspiration. We felt so proud of being an Indian at that moment.

The entire boulevard was lined with cars and other vehicles. The whole of Delhi seemed to have converged in the emerald lawns of India gate. Vendors were the centre of attraction, selling a gamut of things from chuskis to chaat. We walked near the lawns where monkeys performed in front of an eager crowd and children blew up soap bubbles.

'Should I get you an ice cream?' I asked Riya.

She agreed and held my hand tightly as the cold breeze enveloped us. Mohit and Sonam had chaat while we ate ice cream. We sat on the cool lawns licking ice cream and playing a bit of football. The fountains nearby were lit up with coloured lights, making the place seem magical.

We next went to the Amar Jawan Jyoti, which is a burning shrine under the arch of India Gate built to remind the citizens of the soldiers who bravely gave their own lives to uphold the country's honour. We clicked photographs around it. As a new bride looks resplendent when adorned with jewellery, so did India Gate look adorned with yellow lights. I thought about how India Gate was fast becoming the most popular destination to start a campaign, raise awareness against an issue, or protest against government atrocities. It had witnessed quite a few candlelight marches in the past decade alone.

'It's so beautiful here. Such a feeling of serenity and calmness,' I said to Riya while we were sitting in the lawns.

'You make me complete,' said Riya pulling my cheeks and making a complete mess of my hair. I smiled at her.

Mohit and Sonam were roaming around the lawns, hand in hand, while we sat reclined in each other's arms.

We had to reach our guest house and pack our bags for our next destination, so we decided to leave for the guest house shortly.

Mesmerizing Manali

Day 1: Here and there.

We packed our luggage and headed towards ISBT in an autorickshaw. Leaving Delhi seemed difficult, but we were consoled by the fact that on our return journey from Manali, we would eventually have to make a brief stopover at Delhi. Riya and I were in a different autorickshaw which was right behind Sonam and Mohit's. The cold breeze forced Riya to come closer to me. She hugged me and kept her head on my shoulders as we drove towards ISBT. I looked at her eyes and planted a kiss on her lips. It was a gentle kiss, but it still had the burning flame of love. All the way till ISBT, she held on to my hand tightly.

'Jaan, we have reached the bus station. Get up,' I said patting her back as she slept with her head on my shoulders. We got down and headed for the ISBT station. Once there, we kept our luggage on a nearby bench. The person in charge informed us that the last bus to Manali had already left and that we were late. We had no option but to go by another bus which would drop us at Mandi. From Mandi we would have to take another bus to Manali, which is less than hundred kilometres away.

We bought tickets and took our seats. It got increasingly cold as we passed through NH 21. Our bus crossed Kurukshetra and halted briefly at Chandigarh where we had supper.

We were cold to the bone by the time we reached Mandi the next morning. We could hardly stand on our feet and were shivering like hell. Riya and Sonam had wisely worn woollen overcoats and head caps, so they were able to stand the morning chill. Seeing us shiver in the cold, they made fun of us for not having worn woollens. We boarded a bus going to Manali and were off in sometime.

Driving through the winding roads of Himachal Pradesh, we could see snow-capped hilltops from our bus window. It was then that I realized why places like Kashmir and Manali were called heaven on earth. The view was delightful. We drove along the banks river Beas, while I hummed the the song, 'Behti hawa sa tha woh' from the movie *3 Idiots*.

As we got down from the bus, we experienced the first snowfall of our lives. Riya pulled her overcoat closer for warmth and dusted off the snowflakes on her nose. Mohit and I picked up our luggage and went to look for a nice, moderately-priced hotel. We ultimately singled out one for honeymoon couples and booked two rooms. The receptionist handed us the keys while the hotel service boy escorted us to our rooms.

Once in, we walked straight towards the window. The view of the city from our room was breathtaking. The resort was ideally located in the heart of the small town with a breathtaking view of the snow-capped Himalayas. The room felt quaint and personal, with wooden flooring and a fireplace to keep us warm. But the balcony facing the valley was definitely its best feature. We stood in the balcony looking at the town.

Riya brought out a shawl to brave the cold winds. She came and stood close to me, draping the shawl around us. I could feel the warmth of her body as we snuggled together me for warmth. We kissed passionately, exploring each other in pure ecstasy. It was the wildest kiss of my life—on a balcony in freezing cold. We then settled in our room and Riya called for two cups of tea from the hotel restaurant.

Shortly, Mohit and Sonam too joined us. Both seemed to have settled in and had come to our room looking refreshed.

'It's so romantic and the rooms are so cosy,' Sonam smiled and moved closer to Mohit.

I looked at Riya and she abruptly gave me a peck on my cheek. Her sudden outburst of affection every now and then never failed to catch me off guard.

'You will never change, right?' I asked pulling her cheeks.

'You want me to? Don't blame me then if I don't arouse you!' she laughed.

We decided to go to the market to buy some woollen clothes and enquirc about tourist cars. It was slightly warm in the noon as compared to the freezing chill of early morning.

We reached The Mall road which had a few restaurants and garment shops lined on either side. Various tourist guides stood there with maps in their hands. We bought woollen jackets, socks, and gloves. I also bought a bandana for myself. Riya purchased t-shirts for herself and a shawl for her Mom.

'Why don't you purchase something really hot and revealing?' I whispered into her ear.

'Don't worry; I am already carrying them with me,' she giggled.

The temperature dropped down as the daylight dissolved into night. We were shivering even after putting on two sweaters and inners to keep us warm and protected. We went to a restaurant Chopsticks to have dinner. Mohit ordered white rum for everyone.

'Don't' drink so much that we have to carry you to our room,' we told the girls. They were rubbing both their hands to keep warm.

Each one of us had four pegs of rum with dinner.

The momos in particular were delicious. When we came out of the restaurant, it became impossible for us to bear the cold. Riya and I walked back to the resort which was a mere ten minute walk from the restaurant. Sonam and Mohit followed suit.

As we walked together, Riya was so close to me that I could almost feel her breath.

'Let's get naughty tonight. I want to be in your arms, hold you and feel you all over me,' said Riya softly so that Mohit and Sonam could not overhear us.

I gave her a wicked wink.

'Do you know that Manali is famous for weed?' Mohit asked me.

'Yes, I have heard about it, but I am afraid I am not very keen on trying it,' I replied. But Mohit kept insisting we give it a shot.

As we entered the hotel, Mohit said something to the receptionist of the resort. Then he came towards me and told that everything had been arranged for, pointing towards his shirt pocket. I knew it contained weed and asked him how did he manage to get it. He told me not to worry about that and both of us decided to go to my room for our first shot at 'nirvana'. While the girls freshened up, we had fun smoking weed. It gave me an instant high and I was soon feeling drowsy. Riya told us to wrap everything up and Sonam took Mohit with him to their room.

Riya came close to me and moved her finger on my back and then on my thighs. This made me drowsier.

She tried to arouse me, but I was too high to respond to her yearnings.

Fucking hell! I will never try weed, I kept thinking to myself, feeling like I was about to fall off a cliff.

Riya was looking amazing in her nightwear, or so I could tell from my faint vision. I don't remember what happened next.

I woke up late in the morning with a slight headache. By the time I came back to my senses, Riya was by my side, giving me a capsule for my throbbing headache and pouring a hot cup of tea for me.

'You missed last night's fun,' she winked.

'I know. It's okay. I have already planned something special for the coming nights,' I smiled.

'I am having so much fun that even thinking about returning to Mumbai makes me sad. These have been the best days of my life. Let's come here again for our honeymoon,' she suggested. I nodded my head in agreement.

'Do you know how beautiful you look straight out of bed?' I held her close and played with her long earrings.

Mohit came to our room shortly afterwards and told us that Sonam had gone to take a shower and would join us in a bit. Soon we got dressed and left the resort. Taking the Mall road we went to the place where tourist guides generally abound in plenty. We enquired about getting a car on hire and they gave us a two-day plan. We bargained to bring down the cost a little and accepted the offer.

Day 2: Manikaran and Rohtang Pass.

The second day was devoted to Manikaran which was around eighty kilometres away from Manali. We drove along the Parvati valley, driving carefully around the dangerous turns and hairpin bends. We passed through rice fields, shanty tea stalls, herds of goats, and snow-clad mountains.

After a two-hour long journey, we reached Manikaran. A small outlying strip of shopping stalls, street merchants, and eateries told me that we had reached a prime tourist location. We quickly came out of the car and walked across the short span bridge over Parvati River. Along with others, I too was able to breeze down the zigzag lanes after my brief visit to Ram Temple. The sadhus were cooking rice and dal at the edge of the hot springs called 'Vishnu Kund'—the water of which is known to have curative powers. It was surprising for us to see that even in a stretch of cold water, there was a patch which had boiling water.

'This place has something to it. I can feel positive energy all around,' said Riya.

I obviously didn't believe in that, but I knew Riya wouldn't lie. The temple was extremely beautiful and allowed me time to self-introspect and feel the divine power.

'I've heard that if someone takes a bath in the Kund, he would attain salvation,' I told Mohit and Riya while Sonam was still in the temple premises.

We spent some time clicking photographs and seeing the surrounding places. At eleven in the morning, we started our journey to Manali. We halted at a local dhaba where we gorged on some delicious North Indian food.

'I need a smoke,' I announced to the others and excused myself from the group. It was a trick so that I could visit the local gift shop without anybody taking notice. I had to purchase something for Riya as I wanted our night to be a special one.

Riya told me to get back at the earliest as we were getting late and wanted to reach our next destination on time.

Rohtang pass was our next stop. The driver told us that it's the same place where the famous song from *Jab We Met* was shot. Mohit asked us if we could allow him to smoke in the car. Riya and Sonam gave us a tough look and refused, saying boundaries had to be set somewhere. We consented to their request, or shall I say, order. The freezing winds made us grip each other tightly and we didn't even bother what the driver would think. The road was getting bumpier by the minute.

I could not speak due to the freezing weather. The view was gorgeous. At some places, the snow was almost 6 to 8 feet high on both sides of the road. We stopped at a stall which served Maggi.

'Hot Maggi tastes best in cold weather. Even though I am not too much of a Maggi fan, this is just fabulous,' said Mohit.

We agreed in unison. After devouring the plate of Maggi and a simmering hot cup of tea, our vehicle inched its way up the hill. Suddenly, the driver pulled the brakes and stopped abruptly. We saw that in front of us heavy snowfall had covered the road, leading to a dead end. The driver turned to us.

'Look, it is very dangerous to drive ahead from this point onwards. You have to get out and walk. If I drive any further, it can lead to a complete breakdown of the vehicle which can further add to our problems,' he cautioned us.

With no choice left, we got down and clicked a few pictures. We went near the valley and embraced the breathtaking views while having chocolate and biscuits that we were carrying with us. It was very cold and the breeze was biting! We had worn layers of clothing, insulated jackets, even woollen gloves and caps. A pure white sheet of snow had engulfed the entire region. Looking at snowfall while your love is in your arms can't be expressed in words. I was speechless.

Mohit and Sonam went walking a bit further while we chose to stay back and wait.

'What are you thinking?' Riya asked me.

'I was thinking of returning to this place after our marriage. We'll take the Honeymoon Package. I want to spend time at this place with you by my side,' I said holding her hands.

'I am waiting for that day too,' she said. I had planned something elaborate for the night and hoped that Mohit had kept my little secret to himself.

I was just getting my thoughts together when I heard Sonam's voice call out to me.

'What are your plans for tonight?' said Sonam winking at me. Both had returned from their short walk.

I looked towards Mohit with an accusatory glance and he signalled swearing he hadn't told her a thing. I wanted to make my night really special for Riya.

It was getting darker, so we decided to head back home and asked the driver to take us back. That marked the end of day two's sightseeing.

We returned to the Mall road. The driver gave us a lowdown on the next day's plan and left saying that he would be waiting for us outside our hotel on time. Sonam and Riya went back to the hotel while Mohit and I went on a small shopping trip to procure gifts for the girls to make our night more memorable.

I saw a shop which carved names on wooden designs. I asked the staff member to carve Riya's name along with mine on a decorative wooden key ring. Since the girls weren't around, we smoked a couple of cigarettes, after which we returned to our resort.

It was around 7 pm in the evening when we got back to the hotel. The temperature seemed like it had fallen to a chilling minus 2 degrees Celsius. I went to the reception and requested them to send an extra heater in both our rooms.

Riya and Sonam were busy nibbling popcorn and watching TV in Mohit's room. I asked him to keep them engrossed while I managed to arrange everything in our room for a perfect evening with Riya.

'Aadi, where were you? I am so hungry,' exclaimed Riya.

'We will soon have dinner. First, I want you to take a look at this.' I held out my palm and placed a big gift box on it. She looked at Mohit and Sonam to enquire if they were aware of what the gift was. Both reacted as if they didn't know a thing.

She opened the box to find a perfect outfit for the night. I had bought a short black dress for her. Mohit gave me a wicked look that said, *so now I know why you told the receptionist to send one more heater*. Riya was surprised to see the gift as she had least expected it. She jumped off the bed and hugged me. I told her to wear it. Mohit and Sonam realized that we wanted to be left alone, so they made up a silly excuse of going down to the hotel restaurant for a quick bite even though I knew their stomach was full.

'It's a bit chilly outside, so why don't you take this bottle of rum with you for company?' I told Mohit as he was leaving.

Mohit winked at me, as if to wish me good luck, and departed with Sonam.

I went into our room while Riya changed into her new outfit.

'I am in our room. The door is locked. Just knock when you are ready,' I said and left.

After a few minutes, there was a faint knock on the door. I opened it to see Riya standing outside nervously, waiting for my reaction. She looked like a complete bombshell in the dress I had gifted her. It fitted her perfectly, I was speechless. I looked at her from head to toe. She had kept her hair open and they fell loosely on her shoulders. Her black eyeliner highlighted her already pretty eyes. Her glossy lips added colour to her face. She hadn't worn any accessories, which I was glad about, as it would then seem overdone. The dress was a black satin-netted one piece that just about covered her thighs. It had a deep back and a spaghetti strap knot on both sides. My heart skipped a beat. I felt like I had fallen in love with her all over again.

'Why does it feel like the most beautiful girl in the world is with me here in this room?' I smiled and held her hands, leading her into our room.

The main lights had been switched off and replaced by dimmer yellow lights. The room was lit up with decorative candles on the dining table. The trolley beside it had a bottle of Champagne kept in an ice bucket. The trolley was covered with rose petals. The petals had also been sprinkled on the bed, with a bowl of strawberries and chocolate kept right beside it. I played some romantic songs on my laptop to set the mood.

We sat on the dining table facing each other. I opened the champagne and poured us a glass each.

'Cheers to the most beautiful girl in the world,' I said, taking a sip of the drink.

We had our dinner while looking into each other's eyes. None of us spoke a word until she handed me a letter.

'What is this?' I asked her.

'If you can surprise me, so can I. I wrote a little something for you while you were away.'

She got up from the opposite end of the table and came and sat on my lap. Then she kissed my cheeks and kept her hands over my shoulders and continued, 'I want you to read it aloud.'

I opened the letter and read:

I never believed in love at first sight and I still don't, but ours is probably as close as it can get. It all happened quickly, but I am glad we lasted. If at times it seems like I don't care for you, I am sorry. I do care. Every time you are down and troubled, I feel the same way. I try the best I can. I remember how you used to look at me. The charm in your eyes made me fall for you the moment I saw you. You were the first person that ever saw me, the first person to give me hope that I could mean something to someone. Someday, I will marry you and we'll be happy. But right now, we are just too young. And we are still having fun, right? I just wanted to let you know that I'll be yours forever.

I kissed her while she tightened the grip on my shoulders.

Suddenly Riya got up and said, 'I'll be back in two minutes', and went towards the closet.

She came back with her hands behind her and knelt down before me.

'My dear Aadi, will you give me the pleasure of being your wife?' she said holding out a ring towards me.

I was stunned. I never saw this coming. Not at that moment at least.

'My bacchu, you came into my life like a beautiful dream and it seems like I have never woken up from it. I bless the day we met,' said Riya.

Hearing her confess her love to me so earnestly, I was reminded of the day when I first laid my eyes on her. I was scheduled to attend a lecture but as usual, I was wiling away time checking out the girls in my class. Five minutes into the lecture, I heard a girl's voice:

'May I come in sir?'

One look at her and my heart skipped a beat. It was so beautiful, almost like watching a dream. I distinctly remember I had asked myself, 'Is she the one I am looking for?'

She came and sat in the third row and looked back. Our eyes met and in that fleeting second, it was like our souls came together too. We couldn't stop looking at each other. I knew deep down inside that she was indeed the one for me.

And that's the way we met!

We became friends, then best buddies, and now…

'Will you marry me?' asked Riya again.

It was me who had proposed to her a few years back. The memory of that day is still clearly etched in my mind like it all happened yesterday.

We had planned it all out. Swapnil and Sameer were standing in one corner in the garden, ready with what they had been instructed to do. Even I was prepared. As soon as Riya entered, I bent down on my knees, kept the rose in my hand, and said, 'You are my best friend. A friend like you is hard to get. However, a life partner like you for a person like me is impossible.'

I paused for a moment and said, 'Really, I don't deserve a girl like you. I am a flirt. I have the worst image, but still I want to change. I want a girl who can change me. And it's you, my bachha. You are everything to me. You are the love of my life. I love you babe. And every time I see you, I just want to hug you and never let you go. You are special to me. You make me complete. I will never leave you alone in this relationship. Love you. Do you wish to be my beloved?'

She had tears in her eyes—tears of happiness. She just nodded and said, 'I love you too my bachha…love you a lot. Thanks for this moment.'

She accepted the rose. I stood up and we hugged one

another. As soon as we did that, Sameer and Swapnil blew the ribbon and snow spray.

She was overwhelmed with whatever I had done for her. We hugged each other and looked into each other's eyes. Her eyes asked me whether I would be with her forever. My eyes said that I was with her always and forever.

And now she was proposing to me!

'Aadi, what are you thinking about? Here I am proposing to you, and you seem to be on a different planet altogether,' said Riya sensing my thoughts were elsewhere.

'Nothing jaan, just reminiscing about our past,' I said.

She continued, 'It was you who made me realize that I am beautiful, it was you who taught me to live each and every moment of my life. Jaan, you're my world, my every heartbeat—my every breath is for you. Today I have listened to my heart. I have decided to make my feelings known to you. We have been close to each other for quite some time now and I was toying with this idea of proposing to you, but could never find the right moment to do so. I know you were probably expecting me to pop up the question in a grand fashion, but I am too shy to propose to you in public. I have seen you as a perfect boyfriend and now I wish to see you as my perfect husband. So Aditya, WILL YOU MARRY ME?'

I was benumbed. Words failed me. A nervous 'yes'

was all I could say at that moment, as she came over to give me a tight hug.

I touched her back with my fingertips and heard her moan. My hands reached for her knot and untied it to let her dress fall on the floor. I lifted her up in my arms and laid her gently on the bed. She worked her way across my chest, swiftly unbuttoning my shirt and pulling it over my head. As I unzipped my trousers, I took out from its pocket the wooden key ring having our names carved on it. She took it in her hands and kissed it as a drop of tear fell from her eye. I kissed those tears away and gave her a deep kiss on the lips. She moaned in pleasure, returning my kisses with ardour. I took a strawberry and rolled it all over her. She could no longer hold herself, her body rocked with the sensation of pure ecstasy. We ate chocolates while kissing each other and fondled one another for a very long time. I rolled another strawberry in the melted chocolate and passed it on to her. She devoured it instantly, giving me the next piece.

'You are a wild cat in bed,' I whispered in her ear.

"'Shut up, Aadi! I will kill you. By the way, thanks for making my night memorable,' she said, kissing my forehead.

We made love till the crack of dawn. I held her close as we finally drifted off to sleep.

Day 3: Solang Valley.

I got up with an early morning kiss from Riya who was up before me. Sonam came to our room and told us to get ready.

'So how was your night?' Mohit asked while holding Sonam lovingly from behind.

'I think Riya can tell you better. Her nail marks on my body should tell you the story,' I said teasing her as I went to the washroom. I could hear Sonam laughing.

We left our room and called for the driver. We had planned to visit Solang Valley to play snow games and have some fun. It was was hardly a few kilometres away from our resort. The road was the same as that leading to Rohtang Pass. Parachutes in the clear blue sky, dense pine trees, and snow-capped mountains made the sight picture perfect. No wonder Manali is called 'Switzerland' of India. Our trips to Rohtang Pass and Solang Valley proved that right. It was extremely beautiful and offered an enthralling view of the snow-capped Himalayas.

I took out one cigarette from my pack and smoked.

'Now this is what I call having a good time,' said Sonam throwing a snowball at me.

I picked up one and threw it back on her face and she toppled down on the snow losing her balance. She stood up to get back at me but slipped and fell down again. Next was Riya who too slipped trying to help Sonam up. We burst out laughing at the silliness of it all.

Next we decided to try paragliding. A cable car took us to the peak of the mountain along with our pilots carrying a big backpack containing the parachutes. As we moved up, the valley looked like a tiny dot and in a while, we disappeared behind the hills.

As we wore our helmet and harness, we decided to go one by one. I was super nervous, this being my first experience. It knew it would be one hell of a thrilling moment. The pilot gave us the green signal and I started moving ahead along with him. The gear was heavier than I had imagined. After a few steps, I was lifted up above the ground. As we flew in the air, the noise cooled down, the valley looked too small, and the dense pine trees and white snow seemed like a rolled-out carpet. The strong winds helped our parachute to take free falls and gain height in seconds. I could hear Riya and Sonam's screams but couldn't see Mohit anywhere.

As we prepared for the landing, I wished for it to never come to an end. I could feel the speed of falling down. My heart raced twice than normal. Soon everyone landed down safely except for Mohit. We waited for him for sometime but there was no sign of him anywhere. We tried looking for the organizer but he too seemed missing.

We calmed down when we saw Mohit land safely a few feet away. He and the pilot had crashed in the first take off, but in the second, they had been successful.

'It was a thrilling experience! I was so afraid that I kept my eyes tightly shut althrough,' said Riya.

We tried skiing next but I just couldn't get the hang of it. I tried my best but would always topple down after every few steps. It was pathetic! Everyone made fun of me.

Next, we took tickets of the ropeway. Riya and I went behind Sonam and Mohit's cable car. We saw the wonderful view of Manali from 13000 feet above sea level. The cable car was packed and we were comfortably seated. Riya showed me Mohit's cable car, which I hadn't noticed earlier. Both were cuddling even at a height of 13000 feet!

Oh what dangers does love make one take, I thought to myself.

'They look so cute when sitting close to each other.' said Riya pointing towards their cable car just ahead of us.

'Yes, they do! They will soon get engaged once Mohit tells everything to his parents.' I said.

We gave high five to each other and got down from the ropeway with a smile on our faces.

Once back on the ground, Mohit asked us, 'How was the ride?'

We continued laughing and I said, 'The ride was fine, but what we do know is that you surely were having a ball of a time with each other in the cable car.'

Both of them looked at us like small children found eating in the class without the teacher's permission.

We headed back towards the resort.

We first had our dinner and then decided to prepare a bonfire. It was a chilly winter night and the snow glittered on the nearby mountains. We locked our rooms and told the manager of the resort to make special arrangements. We paid him an additional amount for doing so. We asked him to set up the bonfire on the riverbank near our resort. Once set up, Sonam and Mohit sat on the other side of fire exactly in front of us. We could not see the river but could hear its gurgling sound.

We decided to play a game in which each person would have to share his or her most memorable experience in their relationship. We liked the idea and told Sonam to begin.

Sonam looked at Mohit and said, 'I don't know what made me fall for you. I still think about the exact reason why I love you. Was it your looks or your nature? However, whatever it is the fact remains that I love you and I want to marry you soon. I remember how nervous you were when you were at my home with my parents. Your expression told me that you feared rejection. It made me smile then and it still makes me smile now. I can close my eyes and visualize you in the same state. You looked so innocent, even though I can hardly call you that knowing the real you. The moments that we have shared in the past few days will always be close to my heart.'

Next up was Riya who spoke about me.

'I just love watching you and how your eyes sparkle when I am about to say something to you. The glow that appears in them is what I live for. I had many special moments with you but the one that I will cherish for life is when we went to Siddhivinayak temple and took the seven promises. I know you love me more and what you did last night will always remain special to me. I believe people come in your life for a reason, to guide you and help you see yourself. Your presence makes me realize that I am beautiful. Thank you for everything, my sweet little baby. I pray to God everyday to bless you with everything you deserve. I will love you until the end of time.'

I was speechless. I knew she wasn't someone who like to express her feelings very often. I embraced her leaving all the worries behind and thanked her for accepting me wholeheartedly.

I was the next one to speak. I said, 'Everyday, I feel my passion growing for you. I feel that our hearts beat in tandem with each other. Every morning, I look in the mirror and ask myself, "Do I still love Riya the same way as I did when I first met her?" and my reflection always answers back with a resounding "yes". I had heard that love grows stale over time, but with you my darling, the feeling just grows more intense every day. Some love stories cannot be predicted. Ours is one such story but I can assure you our best moment is yet to come. I live for that day and I wish that day will come soon. I want to marry you near the sea, maybe Marine

Drive. I always imagine how, after the ceremony is over, you will sit in the car and I will drive us towards our new home. The girls in our family don't wear Punjabi chuda in marriage, but I want you to wear it. You will be dressed in my favourite red saree with a silver border on it. I will look at the chuda in your hand and smile. You will coyly glance at me and I will smile seeing you blush. All the way while driving, I would think of how beautiful you looked on our wedding night. We will enter our apartment to a new life together. I will wake up by the tinkling sound of your chuda everyday.'

No one spoke anything until Sonam shouted, 'This is so fucking romantic. Mohit, learn something from your friend.'

Riya couldn't resist kissing me after my elaborate description of the wedding day. Sonam and Mohit covered their eyes out of embarrassment.

Mohit was finally the last one to speak. He spoke about Sonam, 'Since day one, we have shared something incredible, something that most people only dream of having in their lives. I had been searching you for all my life. You are sincere, caring, loving, and I wouldn't trade you for the world. I am so thankful and blessed that you loved me as much as I love you. Our life together is amazing now, and together after marriage it will only get better. It may come as a surprise to you, but I have decided that we will fly to Ahmedabad tomorrow and meet my parents. I will introduce you to them so that we can get their approval and proceed with our engagement. We should not hold ourselves from tying the knot. I love you and can't wait to get engaged to you.'

'What? Are you serious? We are supposed to be going back to Delhi tomorrow if you remember,' I shouted along with Riya.

'Tell your parents that your official tour has been extended by two more days. We will fly to Ahmedabad tomorrow and return to Mumbai in two days time. I will not go back to Mumbai before making it official,' exclaimed Mohit.

Sonam stood speechless in one corner, teary eyed. Mohit couldn't hold back his tears either. Both of them hugged tightly and wept. The night turned emotional. The thought of the engagement gave us goosebumps too. I could sense their happiness while they hugged one another—they were really taking it to the next level.

Seeking Approval

The next day, we checked out from the resort, carrying with us the sweet memories of Manali. We took the bus to Delhi, reminiscing about the last three days fondly. *How the days have flown*, I thought boarding the bus.

'I will never forget the night that we spent together in Manali. When we will be old together, I will look back at my life and remember this trip as one of the most memorable,' Riya smiled.

It was a long journey to Delhi. We reached the ISBT bus station after fourteen long hours. From there, we took an autorickshaw to the Delhi Airport.

Once at the airport, I checked our luggage to see if everything was in place before boarding the flight for Ahmedabad. It was then that I realized that my laptop bag was missing.

'Riya, I can't find my laptop bag! If it is lost, I am fucked big time,' I shouted in confusion, still searching for my bag.

'Check again. It must be in your main suitcase,' said Mohit.

'How can you be so careless? You should have checked your bag when we got down from the bus,' said Riya.

I looked everywhere but could not find the bag. Feeling dejected, I boarded the flight along with the rest. They tried to console me and keep me calm throughout the journey to Ahmedabad. But I sat removed from the others, feeling too low to talk. Riya tried her best to console me but to no use. Since it had been a birthday gift from my Mom, it was doubly special to me. I could imagine how terrible she would feel if I told her I had lost it on the trip.

'Don't worry. I will buy a new one for you. Now can you please smile for my sake?' said Riya.

'It's okay. You don't have to buy me a new one. I will manage somehow,' I assured her with a dull face.

'I haven't given you a choice. If I say I will get you one, it means I will. I don't want any discussion over it. Smile now.'

I gave her a half-hearted one. She knew there was no arguing with her over this issue. I had no choice but to agree with her.

We reached Ahmedabad. Mohit's driver was waiting for us outside the airport to take us back in his car. He pointed out Shahi Baug and IIM Ahmedabad to us. Driving through CG road, we reached his house at Paldi. His Mom welcomed us with a gracious 'kemcho'. Her warm greeting made us feel like we had known her for ages even though in actuality, the three of us were meeting her for the first time. I had heard a lot about Gujrati hospitality and how the families are loving and give guests a warm welcome.

Mohit introduced everyone to his Mom and grandmother. We greeted them by touching their feet. His Dad had already retired for the day and was asleep in his room.

After exchanging pleasantries with the elders, Mohit's Mom served us dinner consisting of theplas with pickle.

Then we went inside Mohit's room.

'I love your Mom. She is so sweet,' said Sonam.

'Oh, so you like your new mother-in-law already?' teased Riya. 'Just wait till you guys get married.'

Sonam blushed like a new bride.

After a hectic day, we needed some rest. Mohit and I decided to sleep in the guest room while the girls took the other room. After three nights together, it was hard sleeping away from them.

Tomorrow was a big day, one which would decide the fate of Sonam and Mohit's love story. We slept uneasily that night, not knowing what the new day would bring with it. What would be the ultimate outcome of their fairy tale? A fairy tale that had begun just few months back, and that was now going to be cemented by their engagement. We all waited with eagerness for the day when Mohit and Sonam would officially be declared a couple.

Rahe phoolon ki tarah zindagi aapki,
Chand se bhi haseen ho zindagi aapki,
Kabhi gham ki parchai na pade ye dua hai meri,
Har pal khushiyon se bhari rahe zindagi teri.

Mohit got up before sunrise and woke me up to accompany him for a jog in Parimal Garden. Since his Dad jogged in that particular park every day, Mohit wanted to tell him the truth about his relationship with Sonam there itself. After getting fresh, we left for Parimal Garden on Mohit's bike. His Dad had already left for a park a while back.

Mohit was extremely nervous and repeatedly asked the same question about how his Dad would react. I calmed him down and told him to relax.

Spotting his Dad from afar near the water fountain, Mohit walked towards him and introduced me. His Dad looked like a typical Gujarati businessman.

'Dad, I need to talk about something really important with you,' he said nervously.

'What is the matter, Mohit? Is everything fine at work?' asked his father.

'Yes everything's fine, Dad. I am here with my friends. We took a detour from our business trip to talk about something really important with you. I have been dating Sonam for the past two months and we have now decided to get engaged with your permission. I know it's too soon for you, but you can take your time to think about it. She is the perfect girl for me, Dad. She cares for me and has strong family values. She is a typical Punjabi girl from Delhi,' Mohit said.

'Punjabi? A non-vegetarian? How will she adjust? Didn't you think about these things earlier? I don't want to say anything right now. Let's go home and discuss it,' said Mohit father with a heavy tone.

Mohit remained quiet all the way home.

When we entered the house, we saw that the entire living room was packed to capacity with what looked like Mohit's relatives. I presumed they had been called by his parents to discuss the pressing issue at hand. It looked like a scene straight out of a fish market. Finally, Mohit's father broke the commotion.

'Today's generation, I tell you! We have never restricted you from doing anything in life, have we Mohit? We agreed to all your demands and wishes. Still, you didn't care to inform us about Sonam. You should have at least told your mother about it. You come home and out of the blue tell us that you want to get engaged to her. That's not how it's done,' reproached his Dad.

Mohit remained silent. Sonam and Riya looked visibly afraid to say anything. His Mom tried her best to reason it out with his Dad saying, 'Sonam is a nice girl with strong morals and a sensible head on her shoulders.' But she failed to elicit any kind of favourable response from her husband.

Mohit's Dad gave Sonam his phone and told her to dial the number to her parent's house. Punching in the number, Sonam handed the phone back to him. Taking it, he got up from his place and went to the lawn behind the house. He spoke for around thirty minutes. Occasionally, we peeped outside the window to check what was going on and were somewhat relieved on seeing him smiling. We took it as a good signal, but did not want to unnecessarily jump to any conclusions and get disappointed later on.

He came in and asked Sonam to come with him outside. *What the hell is happening?* I thought to myself. *Why the hell does every love story have a twist! Why can't God make a love story which cruises along smoothly and ends straight at death?*

A few minutes later, Uncle came in with Sonam and announced that he needed some more time to think. All the relatives slowly left for their respective houses.

We all looked at Sonam to enquire about what she was asked, but she kept quiet.

All four of us went into Mohit's room and sat on the bed with tensed minds. His Mom came into our room and gave us the assurance that Uncle would ultimately agree for the marriage and that there was no way he could go against Mohit's decision.

Sonam hugged Mohit's Mom and broke down. The poor girl must be having a hard time with all this. Aunty gently stroked her hair back, and that seemed to have a calming effect on her as her sobs eventually subsided. *Who says mothers-in-law can't be mothers?* I thought seeing them.

Sonam ultimately gave away the discussion she had with Mohit's father. She said the he was mostly worried about her family's living style as compared to their own. He said that the two cultures were vastly different from each other and that it would be very difficult for her to adjust with them. They didn't eat non-vegetarian food at all, and when Mohit wanted to eat it, he had to go outside to do so. Not only that, he also made her understand how Punjabis and Gujaratis have a completely different style of living from each other. And then he left it at that.

Before we could say anything, Uncle entered the room and sat next to Sonam, saying, 'Child, I have never opposed Mohit's decision. If he is happy with this union, I don't mind it. I was just a bit hurt about the fact that he never informed us or even mentioned anything to us on the phone. So the sudden decision to get engaged came as a bit of a shock to us. We don't know anything about you and your family, and we can't decide about our son's future within a second.'

Sonam was already beginning to tear up.

'Now darling, hold onto those precious tears for a little while,' requested Uncle and continued, 'When I went out for a talk with your Dad on the phone, he seemed like a real gentleman and said he would be happy to give away his daughter to Mohit. I told him we were equally lucky to have you as our new daughter. So, all we have to now do is put our heads together and fix a date

for your engagement. But today evening, I have decided
to throw a grand party for our relatives to announce your
engagement. I hope you all are happy now.'

Mohit jumped off from the bed and hugged his
Dad. He touched his parents' feet along with Sonam
to receive their blessings.

Vows to take and prayers to say, promises to be
kept on the engagement day! Tears will be shed when
the rings will be exchanged, and they will be one step
closer to eternal bliss. She will look gorgeous in a bride's
dress. They will dance to the tune of love. Two hands
will embrace forever. Two souls will be fused together
by commitment. Two hearts will join by the purest
form of love.

Sonam was with Mohit's family before the function.
It was just a small party held to announce their
engagement.

The entire house was decorated with flowers. The
atmosphere of the party was vivacious, vibrant, and
lively. Gujarat is known for its liveliness. The house
was slowly flooded with people. I was standing alone
drinking juice and eating ganthias and kachoris. Riya
was with Sonam, while Mohit was getting ready.

Sonam came downstairs with Mohit's Mom and
Riya, with Mohit following closely behind.

Mohit looked dapper in a black suit with a silver
motif on it. But Sonam was indeed the showstopper that
day. All eyes were on her as she descended the stairs.
Even though her outfit was of a lovely colour, and not

the flashy ones that most girls wear on their special day, she still looked stunning. She was wearing a traditional Gujarati sari in red having an intricate pattern of squares in gold woven along its border. I gathered some people whispering that the sari is called Gharchola. It was embellished with heavy sequins all through the pleats, giving it a royal look. Her hair was neatly tied in a side bun, and a heavy dupatta rested on top of her head. She was also wearing a diamond set with matching earrings that added grace to the overall look. An intricate nose ring called 'nath' completed the look. In short, Sonam looked divine.

Riya too looked gorgeous in a pink and silver saree. She spotted me from afar and came and stood beside me. We had snacks and dinner while Sonam was introduced to all the family members one by one. Everyone seemed to take an instant liking to her. And since no party in Gujarat is complete without Garba, we all were asked to join in as the music echoed. I was the worse at it, while Riya danced like a pro and tried teaching me a few moves. I didn't even want to participate but Mohit forced me to do so. Occasionally, Riya looked at me and laughed seeing my awkwardness. Finally, the party drew to a close.

'Beta, we welcome you in our family with open arms. We'll take care of you the same way your parents did for so many years. You can share everything with us and please think of us as your parents and not your in-laws,' said Mohit's Mom affectionately. Mohit's Mom assured her that she will be a daughter to their family, not a daughter-in-law.

Sonam couldn't stop her tears. When a girl leaves her parents with whom she has stayed all her life and enters a completely new family, she hopes of receiving the same love and affection from them. With Sonam, it was no different.

I thought of how she was such a lucky girl to get such a supportive family. I hugged Mohit and congratulated him on the engagement.

We left for Mumbai the next day. We had to join our offices and report to our manager with an application for taking extended leaves. Both Sonam's and Mohit's parents had decided that they would meet in a week or two and decide the engagement date. It was not possible for Mohit and Sonam to join them due to work. Moreover, both of them wanted to let their parents meet alone. We landed in Mumbai after an eventful week. But my thoughts kept going back to Riya and our future togrther. Would our love story walk the same path as Mohit's and Sonam's? Or would there be something unpredictable, something which could change the course of our paths entirely? Few things are better left unsaid!

A Few Things Left Unsaid

Once we reached Mumbai, we headed straight for our respective offices and gave notices about our extended leaves. A reasonable excuse about missing our scheduled flight, with no flight for the next two days in snow covered Manali, did the trick for us. Riya couldn't come up with an excuse and so she got a warning letter from her HR department. But it didn't hamper her incentives or job profile. I consoled her and told her to take it easy.

After a hectic day at office, we left for our respective homes.

'Aditya, where is your laptop? I was unpacking your bag and realized that it was missing,' Mom asked me.

'I have given it for servicing. They will return it in few days,' I lied, trying to dodge the question for the moment.

I found myself overwhelmed with a sense of shame.

The next day, Riya informed me that she had purchased a brand new Acer laptop for me worth eighteen thousand rupees. I screamed at her for having spent that entire amount without even once consulting me.

'Jaan, you know how your family is hard pressed for money. You should not have spent that big an amount. The trip cost us a bit of money too and going ahead and blowing up that entire amount on a laptop is not right. We have already spent a lot of money in the last few days,' I reasoned with her, but she got angry at my sudden outburst.

'You don't care that I bought it with so much love? Here you are bombarding me with your logic when all I did was buy you a new laptop so that your work doesn't suffer,' she replied.

She left without saying another a word. I never intended to hurt her. I just cared for her family and didn't want her to be scolded for pampering me without thinking the least bit about them.

She refused to take my calls the next day nor did she meet me at our regular meeting time outside her office. I knew she was supposed to be going for an office party, but would she be going at all after our little argument? She called me to tell me that she was indeed going for the party and that I should not call her or chase her there. I felt utterly dejected.

Mohit called me after some time.

'Aditya, I am so sorry. God! I am such an idiot. I hadn't opened my luggage since returning to Mumbai as I was busy answering congratulatory calls from relatives. I opened the bag right now to find your laptop inside it. I must have put it in there by mistake in a hurry while checking out of the hotel,' said Mohit in an apologetic tone.

'Oh God. And just when Riya got me a new laptop! I have already angered Riya with my scolding and now this discovery. This can't be happening to me,' I said and kept the phone.

I called up Riya immediately. She didn't pick up as expected. I tried again but to no avail. I kept on blaming myself for the foolishness. I felt bad that Riya had spent all that money on the laptop unnecessarily. But who can predict the future?

I called her again. This time she picked up. Her voice sounded like she had consumed far too many drinks at the party. She shouted at me over the phone when I told her my old laptop had been found in Mohit's bag and hung up without listening to anything I had to say!

Later in the night, I got a message from her. *From now on, please don't message me or call me. The sight of your face irritates me. In fact, everything you do irritates me. Don't do all this drama in front of me, trying to sound apologetic and all.*

I messaged her back saying, *I never put up a show, dear. Please, I am really sorry. Cross my heart. I swear never to repeat this. Please give me one last chance.*

I got an instant reply from her saying, *Please stop doing all this. Today you have hurt me a lot. Money doesn't matter to me. What matters is your trust, which you broke today like a piece of glass.*

I messaged back saying, *What are you accusing me of? I merely got confused. I forgot that I had given my laptop to him. I am sorry. Please. Can't you understand just how sorry I am?*

She replied, *Please. Even after knowing me for the last few years you can say that I am lying, then I was a fool to love you so much. You can never change. Fate brought us together again and we were so happy. Why did you have to do this? Now you are confused. You took revenge. You never wanted me back. My Mom scolded me like hell for having spent all that money on a laptop! I know what I went through for your eighteen thousand rupees.*

I could not understand why she was saying all this. So I called her up instead. She took a long time to pick up her phone and when she did, I could tell she was still at the party as there was music being played in the background. She seemed to be drunk and by the gibberish she spoke, I could tell she was not in her correct state of mind.

'Can you stop drinking? I know that you are with your colleagues and must have joined in their drunken revelry. But, please, don't cross your limits. Just go home and sleep,' I said shouting at her so that she may take me seriously.

She agreed and returned home. I called her up to confirm and only once she reached home did I breathe a sigh of relief.

Sometimes I close my eyes to imagine how it would be if everything were perfect! I loved her and knew that she loved me and cared for me. No relationship is complete without its fair share of fights.

The next morning when I got up, I saw a message from Riya that brought a huge smile to my face.

I am so sorry for behaving so badly last night. I was drunk and don't remember a word I was saying. If I hurt you yesterday, it was done unintentionally. I know it was a stupid thing to do, but I was really not in my senses. I love you so much but when you are careless, it drives me nuts. When you speak about my past, it hurts me. I know you don't mean anything by it, but I am so insecure when it comes to your love. I don't want to lose you again. I realize you can have any girl in the world, but you chose me. And I am not going to let a silly fight come between us.

Is there any way I can make it up to you? I hope you have it in your heart to forgive me. You've no idea how much I have missed you all these days.

Love you a lot!

I called her up and we decided to meet after our office hours.

I was desperately waiting for the shift to end. It feels so nice when you make up or kiss your girlfriend or boyfriend after a long fight. It had been three days that we hadn't talked to each other, neither had we met. I went to her office after my shift got over and when she came out, I rushed to give her a tight hug. She couldn't hold back her tears and ran towards me, clinging to me tightly. We kissed each other and looked into each other's eyes. I could see the pain of missing me in her eyes.

'Aadi, I have made the decision of telling my Mom about you and about our wish to get engaged,' she said.

Goodness gracious! Was she serious?

'Your Mom has a hint about our relation and she knows that you love me. However, my Mom still doesn't have a clear idea about what we are up to. I will try and convince her to accept our relationship and take it forward with my father,' Riya said as we headed towards her home, hand in hand.

'Don't you think it's too early? I doubt your Mom will accept our relationship so easily,' I said knowing how strict her family was.

She assured me that she wouldn't do anything silly and make her Mom understand. It made me utterly nervous. I was not afraid to face her Mom if the situation demanded it. However, I was afraid of losing my love. We had seen many difficulties in our relationship until now and I wanted a smooth journey ahead. Not everyone is as lucky as Mohit and Sonam. We had tried to and had managed to come so far. We managed to maintain the passion and intensity in our relationship even after so many years. We didn't let it be monotonous. We kept the spark of love alive.

They were about to tie the knot after seeking the blessings of their parents. We did not know if the same future lay ahead for us. But life never is so easy and predictable, is it? Will it be a smooth journey ahead or a roller coaster ride?

We were keeping our fingers crossed!

When I reached home that night, I logged in to my gmail account to check for unread mails. I saw Riya online, so we started chatting.

Aadi, I am very nervous. I don't know what my Mom's reaction will be. I don't want to lose you again, popped her message.

Don't be nervous. When you will speak with your Mom, be confident else, your nervousness will reflect in your tone. God is with us. Don't you say this often? I typed.

But I am still afraid about her reaction. Tell me something to calm me down, she said.

If I were in your place, I would have held you tight, taken you to my Mom and said, 'Mom, she is my wife. I hope you don't mind. Even if you do, she still will be my wife! So the best thing for you will be to accept her with open arms, I punched in.

Stop it, Aadi! I will kick your...

Come on, go ahead. Finish your sentence. Kick your what? I said cheekily.

I will kill you. Bye. I am logging out. I will tell my Mom tomorrow morning when I get up. Love you.

With that we came to the end of our online chat. All I could do was wait for the next day to know what transpired at Riya's home.

The next day, Riya told me about her conversation with her Mom.

She told me that she had woken up early in the morning, not having had much sleep due to a tense state of mind. She had gone into the kitchen where her Mom was preparing breakfast. She went and stood behind her without speaking a word. Her Mom turned around to find Riya standing right at the entrance of the kitchen. She saw that Riya was nervous and asked if she wanted to speak about something. Riya told her Mom to follow her into the room as she wanted to speak to her on a very important topic.

They sat on the bed facing each other.

'Mom, I want to speak to you about my future. I know it's too early and I am not old enough to be speaking on this topic, but I will try and hope that you understand my point of view,' said Riya.

'What are you talking about, my dear? Is there any problem?' she enquired.

'No Mom, there is no problem as such. But I...

Actually... You know... I want to talk to you about Aditya. We want to be engaged. We won't marry anytime soon. However, we wanted to get your seal of approval and take our relationship one step ahead.'

'What are you saying? Are you in your right senses? You know what the condition of our family is. Dad is still not over the loss we suffered in our business. We are struggling to make ends meet here. We have the responsibility of your brother's education as well as running the house with the salary that you get. I think it is too early for you to be thinking about such things,' she said in a fit of anger.

She kept quiet for some time after which she told her, 'I am not asking you to arrange a grand function for our engagement. I am not even asking you to call all our relatives. However, we can manage a small family function and proceed with it.'

'You are being selfish here and thinking of just yourself. Why can you not think of your brother? For once, think about him and his education. Your father is already in a trauma, and if we discuss these things in front of him, then God knows what will happen. Try to understand, dear. I am not against you or your relationship with Aditya. I know that he is a nice guy and will keep you happy. However, I also know that he is not stable financially and will not be able to provide for your well being. Let him get somewhere in life and maybe then we can talk,' she advised.

'I still don't understand what problem it will create.

It's not like after marriage I will stop thinking about my brother and my family. I obviously care for you and Dad. But I don't want to lose Aditya. Please try and understand,' Riya pleaded with her.

'I do understand your feelings. I have told you this before that I am not against you and your relationship. However, this is not the right time to speak about this. You both need time to get settled and have your own identities. You have some responsibilities to fulfil. Once your priorities are done with, we can surely think about Aditya. I hope you won't talk about this again, especially in front of your Dad. He has too much on his plate already,' she said.

'Forget it. You will never understand me. I have told you so many times that I won't stop caring for my family. You are my first priority, I very well know that. But there is nothing wrong in taking our relationship one step ahead at this point. So fine, if you don't want me to talk about this again, I won't,' said Riya.

And that's how it all ended.

I told Riya that I wasn't surprised by the outcome and said that I had expected this to happen.

'Don't be upset, jaan. Your Mom is not against our relationship. She just doesn't think it is the right time for us to get engaged. At least she didn't reject it outright. Please don't cry. I am not going anywhere, so please smile. You look pathetic when you cry,' I said trying to make her smile.

Love is a pain which keeps burning inside you. That burning feeling keeps a person alive. We lived for each other and dreamt a lovely life with each other. Not having my expectations met hurt me. But I kept the hurt within myself and prepared to face another day.

A Secret Marriage

Come soon near Inorbit Mall, Malad, Mohit messaged me. I called Riya to tell her that Mohit had asked me to meet him at the mall. She told me that Sonam had sent her the same message. I was near Malad and reached the mall directly. I called Mohit to enquire where he was. He told me that he was waiting at Pizza Hut with Sonam. Riya hadn't reached yet. She was on her way to Malad.

'What happened? Is it something urgent?' I asked while sitting on the couch.

'Let Riya come. We will tell you then,' said Sonam.

I ordered one spicy veggie pizza for myself. We talked about general stuff until Riya came. She asked the same question that I did.

'I don't understand why you have both called us at the same time at the same place? What is it guys?' I asked with curiosity.

They smiled looking at each other and Mohit gave Sonam the eye nod to reveal the suspense.

Finally, Sonam said, 'We have called you here for a special reason. Just this morning, my Dad called to tell me that Mohit's family and they have decided the engagement date. It has been set for March 3. We have to leave after some days for the preparations.'

'Wow! This is awesome news. Congratulations to both of you. I can't express my happiness. This calls for a party. I still can't believe it is happening so fast. I remember the day you both met for the first time, and today your engagement date has been fixed. We are really happy for you guys,' I congratulated them on behalf of both Riya and me.

'We are leaving in some days' time because there are a whole lot of preparations remaining and even the invitations have not been sent out yet,' said Sonam.

Mohit was leaving for Gujarat while Sonam was going to Delhi in the coming days. The engagement date was nearing and they had to plan and implement many things. They had booked their tickets and were ready to leave for their respective homes. This was one love story that didn't have any twists and turns by God's grace. But I knew such a perfect story is a rare case.

I suggested that they throw a party just for friends before leaving. But Riya was not particularly excited about it. I suppose I knew the reason. Before I could speak, Mohit asked her why her mood was low.

She told him about her showdown with her mother regarding the engagement. I felt bad but helpless. I took her in my arms and told her all would be okay. Sonam too got up from her chair and sat on our couch, trying to make Riya understand.

'Riya, you are harbouring a misconception in your mind. Your Mom did say that Aadi is a nice guy and that she would think about it in the near future. So why are you thinking so much about it? You should be happy that she has at least agreed to think over it. If she had any problems regarding you and Aditya, then she would have stopped you from seeing him altogether. She wouldn't have encouraged your relationship,' Sonam added.

I could tell Riya saw light in her argument, but she was still doubtful. 'You don't understand, Sonam. No one does. I have felt the pain of losing him before. I can't afford to lose him. I know that I have to take care of my family, but that should not come in the way of my marriage. I can't get a guy who will love me so much and accept me as I am. I have seen darker sides of life. It is not easy to be in the world all by yourself,' said Riya trying to hold back her tears.

Mohit got out his mobile phone from his jeans and showed a message to Riya. It was the message I had sent him the night before.

I was so happy today that Riya will be telling her Mom about our relationship. But I think luck will never favour me. Her Mom rejected me as an unsuitable groom owing to the fact that I am just starting out in life and will not be able to support a family economically at this stage. She is not wrong on her part. And I always expected this to happen. I feel bad for Riya. She really cares a lot for me and I know she would be depressed after this incident. I managed to make her understand that we will always be together and that no one can separate us, but it hurts me to see her so upset. I hope she gets over this and moves on. If it was in my hands, I would have married her today itself. She is a sweetheart. Sorry to disturb you, but I wanted to share my feelings with someone.

I don't know what overcame Riya at the moment, but she suddenly got up and exclaimed, 'Let's get married.'

'Jaan, we are already married. I hope you remember our seven promises,' I teased her.

'That was unofficial. Let's make it official. I am serious,' she said.

'Have you gone nuts? What are you talking about? I was just kidding with you. Is getting married so easy?' I was not in a mood to joke anymore.

'It is. If you love me, then stop arguing. We won't tell anyone. We will keep it a secret. Let's have a court marriage.'

Everyone was shocked. Mohit stared at me while Sonam gave a hard look to Riya.

'This is not a piece of cake. It's marriage. Don't you understand? It's marriage, for God's sake!' chided Sonam.

A long silence engulfed the room No one spoke. I was speechless. I felt like someone had banged an iron rod on my head. *Was it a dream or a nightmare?*

Aditya gets married to Riya officially. A secret marriage. Wake up. This is real life, not reel life!

'Riya, you think it is easy? What if your parents come to know of it later on, maybe one or two years down the line? I know you both love each other and I can understand what you are feeling right now. But that doesn't mean you will take a bad decision now and regret it for the rest of your life,' said Sonam.

Riya was firm with her decision. I knew she could do crazy things, but never thought just how crazy.

'No one will know. We can keep it a secret. And we are eligible for marriage, so what's the problem here? No one can take legal action against us for getting married. Heck, no one will even know we are married,' said Riya. I could see how excited she was at the prospect of getting married secretly, making it a big cause of worry for me.

Mohit, who had remained quiet until then, said, 'Riya, do you trust Aditya? If you trust him and have faith in him, then stay calm. Your family needs your attention now and if you take such steps, they may lead to several other problems in your life ahead.'

'You may do all the explaining you want, but I stand firm on my decision. At least we can think over it Aadi,' she pleaded with me. I agreed to give it a thought only so that she could forget talking about it for a while.

'Guys, if you are serious, then let me tell you that we are not here after fifteen days. So be careful. Don't take unnecessary risks. We are sorry but it's not possible for us to wait,' said Sonam.

We smiled and told them to enjoy. We assured them that we would be careful enough not to hurt anyone's feelings. This was not so serious since no third party was involved. We both could resolve the issue on our own. We departed for our offices after the brief lunch session.

That night was again an uneasy one for me. Did Riya really want to get married in secret? I loved her. I loved her beyond imagination. We had overcome many obstacles along the way, and if at this juncture in our relationship she wanted to get married, why was I taking a step back? AND THEN IT STRUCK ME. We can't keep on waiting for her parent's approval any further. And what guarantee was there that if I waited for their approval, they wouldn't attempt to get her married off to someone else? In that split second, I decided to marry Riya. That time officially!

Suddenly the world seemed to be a perfect place, a place for Riya and me to spend the rest of our lives together in total bliss, without difficult parents by our sides.

I met Sameer and discussed everything with him. He was shocked to hear about me having a change of heart and deciding to marry. I told him to be the first witness and another office colleague to be the second witness from my side. We had to apply in the registration office first, but I informed Sameer much prior to the date for confirmation. The next day we went to the registration office, applied for marriage, and completed all the necessary documentation work.

The officer there said, 'We will put up your names on our notice board around fifteen days from now. Then you will get the date of marriage. If in those fifteen days anyone raises an objection to your marriage, then we can't proceed with the rest.'

We agreed and came out of the office. I couldn't believe that within a month's time, we would be getting married.

The fifteen days passed by in a blur. When we saw our names displayed on the notice board, our happiness knew no limits. We had dreamed about it for so long that it took us time to understand the enormity of the situation. We lived each day to be the one for each other. All our memories flashed in front of my eyes when we were staring at each other.

'I still can't believe that we are getting married. Pinch me. I hope it's not a dream,' I said.

She pinched me and I screamed out aloud, making people on the streets turn their heads to see what was causing so much noise. We went shopping the next weekend in preparation for our court marriage. Riya purchased a gorgeous sari for herself with zardosi work on it. As per my wish, she purchased a Punjabi chuda too. Wearing the bangles is not part of our tradition, but it was always my wish to see her wearing them. She got our name engrained on them as per the custom.

Everything was prepared. We bought rings too. The rings that would bind us in responsibilities. They will stand testimony to our promise of standing by each other's side forever and would make us realize our limitations. But most important of all, they would make us realize our love for each other.

'You look good in your sherwani,' said Riya when I tried on the outfit for her.

I didn't know how I looked. I didn't care how I looked. What mattered to me was that I was looking good for Riya and that she was happy. We waited for the day to arrive. I was finally going to marry the girl of my dreams!

Finally, there was just one day left before our wedding. The date of our marriage had been fixed for February 22, just missing Valentine's Day by a week.

I called Sameer to remind him to be there as a witness on time. He asked me whether I was nervous or excited. I told him even I didn't know the answer. It was a feeling of mixed emotions. The night seemed never ending. My heart was pacing so fast, I could count the heartbeats on my fingers. Just when I was thinking what was going on in Riya's mind, she messaged me,

Tomorrow night will be our first wedding night. However, we will be away from each other. Love you, my darling!

A Twist in the Tale

The day of my wedding finally arrived. I took my new sherwani and went to Mohit's flat as I couldn't wear it in my house for fear of arousing suspicion among my parents. Mohit was not in Mumbai but I had keys to his flat. I went there and changed into the sherwani, which was cream in colour and had silver work on it. I looked at myself in the mirror and took a long breath. Probably this was the last time I was looking into the mirror as a bachelor. I smiled. No boundaries could separate us now. The anxiety was finally over. I took a cab to the registration office. I called Riya but she didn't pick up the call. *She must be busy getting ready*, I thought to myself and headed out.

While driving the car on my way to the registration office, I recalled again the day when I saw Riya for the first time. Time brought us together and one fine day, I proposed to her and she accepted my love with grace. Still destiny had something else planned for us. We met again and this time we were very sure that we wanted to be with each other for good. From this day forward, she would not walk alone. My heart will be her shelter and my arms will be her home.

I reached the registration office. Sameer and my office colleague came within a few minutes. It was a pleasant morning, and I could not wait to see Riya in a bride's sari. I wanted to see her wearing the chuda on her wrists, which she had decided to wear just to see me happy. I was excited and could barely contain my emotions.

Sameer patted me on my back said, 'I have known you for years, but this is the first time I have seen such a huge smile on your face.'

'I never expected us to get married so early. Never in my wildest dreams. And to see our dream finally coming true is just unbelievable, Sameer,' I exclaimed.

'I can understand your feelings, buddy. I remember the way you would drink alcohol just to garner a bit of attention from her. Today, you will finally marry her,' said Sameer.

Sameer said that he had written a note for both Riya and me to mark this beautiful day. He took out a sheet of paper from his pocket and started reading.

Lady luck made you meet Riya in college and you both fell in love with each other. You have been together for many years now and all I have to say is that two people couldn't have been more perfect for each other. I just want to wish you good luck for the future. You make for a lovely couple and I am proud to be here with you as a witness and a friend on your wedding day.

I was overwhelmed by his kindness. He has indeed been a good friend to me over the years and a worthy choice for the best man at our wedding.

I looked at my watch and saw that Riya was running late. She should have been here by now. I was worried whether everything was okay at her home. There wasn't much traffic from her place to the registration office, so she should have easily made it here. I dialled her number but she didn't respond. I was getting uncomfortable now.

The clock struck twelve in the afternoon. We were already late. I couldn't understand the reason behind her delay. I didn't want to call Mohit, but I had no option.

'Hey Mohit, How are you buddy?' I asked him.

'I am fine. Just a little occupied with work. How have you been, lucky boy? So you are officially getting married before us. Congratulations on reaching the end of bachelorhood.'

I wanted to tell him that Riya had not reached yet but he seemed so enthusiastic about our marriage that I did not want him to be worried unnecessarily.

'Yes, I know it's the end of bachelorhood. But Mohit, listen. I have called you up for another reason. Can you please tell Sonam to call Riya and check where she is? She has not reached the registration office yet. She should have been here by now. She is not picking my calls either. Can you tell Sonam to call her or her landline number?' I said in a dejected tone.

'Don't worry. I will tell Sonam to call her up and find out what is causing the delay. She will give you a call in fifteen minutes or so and update you with the status. Chill, my boy!' he said and kept the phone down.

Those fiteen minutes seemed like they would never end. Sameer was as worried as me. I kept telling myself to try and remain calm, pushing all the negative thoughts away. I felt alone, even in Sameeer's presence. I messaged and called Riya several times but she didn't respond.

Finally my phone rang. I quickly retrieved my cell phone from my pocket. It was Sonam. My happiness vanished within a flash and I suddenly became a bundle of nerves.

'Aditya, I tried calling her several times on her mobile but she didn't pick up my call. I called her on the landline number too, but no one picked up. I don't understand what has happened. There could be some problem or she might be on the way. Do wait for some time and give me a call if she comes,' said a tensed sounding Sonam.

I had no option but to wait. The court timing was till 4 pm. I was completely broken. I knew she wouldn't betray me this time. I trusted her, I trusted her a lot. This was just so unexpected. I had planned the wedding night and along with it, so many surprises for her. I had so many dreams, but everything seemed futile now. I called her again but still there was no response.

She is not coming, I told myself. Finally, I decided to leave. A broken heart gives way to deeper fears. I thought I had lost her forever. How could this end so suddenly? In the absence of her love, my happiness has vanished. For all the times we laughed, for all the times we hugged and kissed, and for all the times we made sweet love, I can never get over her. I used to love her so much, I used to adore her, but the ending is not what I expected.

I reached home without realizing I was still wearing the sherwani.

Mom asked me where had I gone dressed like that and what was I up to. I could not hide my pain any longer and told her every single truth about our love story. I told her the plans we made together and the decisions we took to live with each other. Like any other Mom would have done, she was extremely hurt that I had lied to her.

I wept in front of her trying to make her understand my situation. I told her I needed her support. She hugged me and told me everything was going to be okay. I retired to my room hurt, refusing to eat anything and smoking endless cigarettes. *How could you have done this to me, Riya? I love you.* I shouted and screamed, if only she would hear.

Somewhere in my heart, I knew she couldn't betray me. She loved me. She cared for me. She would always tell me that she loved me more than I loved her. She would not do this without informing me; I sensed there was something fishy. I decided to go to her house and see for myself what exactly the issue was.

She can't lose interest in me so suddenly. She can't love anyone else.

Wiping the tears off my face, I started my bike and zoomed off to her house. The silence filled the evening even in noisy traffic. I could not hear anything. All I could hear was Riya saying, *Tomorrow night will be our first wedding night. However, we will be away from each other. Love you, my darling!*

Her last message to me hammered in my head all the way till I reached her apartment. As I climbed up the stairs, my heartbeats increased. Standing outside her apartment door, I suddenly got cold feet.

It was then that I noticed a couple of shoes and slippers lying about outside her doorstep. In my head, I already feared the worst. Just then, an Uncle came outside the apartment. He was dressed in white clothes. I mustered the courage to ask him what was happening inside. He put one hand on my shoulders and told me in a soft voice that Mr Umesh, Riya's father, had breathed his last that morning.

I stood there stunned. *It was impossible. It was just impossible.*

How could this happen all of a sudden? And why hadn't Riya informed me about it?

I rushed into her apartment but could see neither Riya nor her Mom. Riya's brother was crying on a relative's shoulder. Everyone had tears in their eyes. I was shocked to see the glumness of it all. I couldn't believe my eyes.

I asked one lady how it had happened so suddenly. However, she did not know anything. Then a screeching siren of an ambulance filled the air. I ran downstairs and stood near the entrance of her society. As the ambulance approached towards her gate, I felt my heart getting heavy and my body getting cold. The ambulance stopped inside the gate. Riya and her Mom came outside. Riya still didn't see me. They both were crying loudly. I could feel their pain. I still hadn't accepted the fact that Riya's Dad had left the world so suddenly.

The hospital staff took the body out of the ambulance. I was not able to react nor did I have courage to approach Riya. A few men from the family came forward and took the body upstairs. It was then that Riya saw me. She stood still for a minute. She had stopped crying and just stared at me. I had never faced a situation like this and was completely unaware of how I should react. She came close to me with heavy steps. We didn't utter a word. We both stared at each other for some time. Then Riya embraced me and wept like a small girl. The entire apartment resonated with her sobs.

'Riya, how did this happen?' I asked her.

'It was just so sudden. I was not in a state to inform anyone. I still can't digest the fact that he is not amid us anymore. I loved him so much,' she cried loudly.

All the relatives gathered around to pay their condolences. Riya told me what exactly happened.

'After I messaged you last night, I went to sleep. I was so excited about our marriage that I got up very early to get ready. At the breakfast table, Mom told me that Dad was not feeling particularly well. He was sweating a lot since morning and had complained of shortness of breath. We didn't want to take a chance with his health as he was suffering from hypertension since the past few days. We took him to the nearby hospital and got him checked upon by the doctor who asked his staff to keep Dad under observation until evening. I was by his side the whole time. Whenever I thought of messaging or calling you up, someone would invariably call my name. I went to the washroom to freshen up. When I came back from the washroom, I saw something abnormal and informed doctors immediately. They came and injected him. Mom rushed to the hospital. She had gone home to bring food for him. After some time, the doctor came and said that he had a heart attack and that they could not do anything to rescue him in time. It was so hard to believe that he had left us and would never return,' said a weeping Riya.

I gently stroked her hair, trying my best to comfort her.

She continued, 'He was the one who taught me to walk; he was the one who stood beside me in my bad times. He was my world. He was my life. It was so hard for him that even at the last minute he looked at me. He tried to open his eyes wide but they shut forever. He tried to tell me to take care of Mom and my brother. He tried to reach for me; he wanted to hold my hand. He wanted to hug me for the last time. However, he couldn't. He let his little girl be alone in this unknown world. He won't be with me to hold my hand or catch me when I fall. He has left us forever. My life has come to a screeching halt. I want to ask God why he has done this to us. Why did he take away one thing that mattered the most to me? Why always me? I want my Dad back. I want him to sit beside me when I get married. I want him to hug me when I leave this house and come to yours. I want him to just be there with me at all times.'

Riya cried and cried till her tears dried out. I tried to tell her that the body may have run its course, but the soul lives on forever.

The Saviour

The next day, I called Mohit to inform him about the tragedy.

'Hey buddy, how was your wedding night? You got up early?' He laughed. He certainly was not aware of the situation.

'Mohit, you won't believe this, but things are not the same anymore. The reason why Riya couldn't come for the marriage yesterday was because her Dad has expired,' I said in a heavy tone.

Mohit couldn't believe it. I told him everything that had happened yesterday and asked him to call Riya up and see how she was doing. I called Sonam too and told her the same thing. Both of them were about to postpone their engagement but I told them not to do so. Both Riya and my plans of attending their engagement seemed dicey now. It was impossible for Riya to attend it and I didn't want to leave her alone. I convinced both of them not to postpone the engagement even if we couldn't turn up. Both agreed to go ahead with it, but with a heavy heart. Riya messaged me that Sonam and Mohit had called her. She felt bad that she would not be able to attend their engagement. I told her to take care of herself and her Mom. I felt extremely sad for her brother. He was still so young and had a long life ahead.

As the days passed, our conversations got shorter and shorter. We would talk for a few minutes and I would tell her to keep wading through the waters till she reached the shore. In her family, it's not allowed to speak on the phone a lot or even step out of the house for a few days after someone's death without any specific reason. She had taken leave from her office for a few days. Three days passed and it was my birthday. I remembered how happy I had been on my last birthday with Riya. This time, happiness evaded us. I woke up to receive a message from Riya on my phone.

Many many happy returns of the day! I am sorry that I can't be with you on your birthday. You may think that I don't miss you and I don't think of you as much as I did earlier. However, I want to tell you today that with every passing minute, I think of you. Today even if I am not with you, just close your eyes and you will find me standing there. I will always be with you and support you. Enjoy your day and don't be sad. I know you are upset, I know you felt equally bad but today is your day, so enjoy it. Your family wants to see you happy. Be happy for my sake, please.

She was the best! She understood exactly how I felt. She understood every emotion in me. No one could understand me better than Riya.

I spent the day with my family. My Mom sensed that I was upset. When no one was in my room, she came to me and asked me what happened after that incident.

'Mom, the reason why Riya didn't turn up that day was not because of her attempt to betray me or because she had hard feelings towards me. It was because her Dad had passed away. They were already under a financial crisis and this has made things worse. She is completely broken and needs my support,' I cried.

She sat down and told me to come over and lay my head her lap. She told me that Riya's family was her first priority and told me not to impose any decisions on her. She had many responsibilities on her plate now, including her brother. I could see sense in my mother's talk.

I kissed her cheek and told her she was the best before retiring off to bed.

My performance in the office was also adversely affected. It was the month where maximum incentives were given out to employees. In no way was I in the contention owing to my poor performance. I could not even complete my basic targets. Every now and then, I was concerned about Riya's health and her condition. I did not tell her what I was going through in office as I did not want to burden her further with my problems too. We could not talk often due to all the relatives who had assembled at her home for the rituals that are conducted in the first fourteen days following someone's death.

My manager warned me about my performance. This time Mohit was not there to defend me and that made the situation worse. My stats were poor. My poor performance affected my health and I suffered from regular headaches. Each day without Riya kept getting more and more difficult for me. I remained aloof most of the time, even in the office premises. I used to complete my office hours and leave straight for home without socializing.

Sameer called me that evening and asked me whether I could meet him. I wanted someone with whom I could share my feelings. I met him and cried a lot on his shoulders. He was the one who supported me in all my bad times. I wished Sonam and Mohit could have been with us. He told me to be strong and support Riya in this time of need. I finally managed to smile. After a long time, I had shared my feelings with someone and felt relaxed that day. I thanked Sameer for being there.

My phone rang. It was Riya.

'Aadi, I am joining office from tomorrow. I can't take so many days off. My office timing is till 6 pm. You think you can meet me after the shift?'

'Sure. I hope you are okay now. Are you in a condition to join office?' I asked.

She said she was fine and that joining office would do her good as it would divert her mind from the gloomy atmosphere at home. Her voice too seemed much better than before.

Finally, we were meeting each other. Finally, I would see my love after almost half a month. This brought a smile on my face. I waited for her shift to get over. My shift got over two hours before hers. I saw her walking from a long distance. It felt so nice to see her. Just looking at her made me feel content. I closed my eyes and thanked God for having taken care of her in my absence.

She came and stood in front of me. I glanced at her. She looked pale. The twinkle in her eyes had vanished. The dark circles under her eyes were clearly visible. She had lost weight too. She seemed very tired from her voice. She somehow managed a weak smile and sat on my bike. We drove to Grant lane, one of our favourite places from our dating days. We had special memories associated with that particular lane.

When we reached there, she hugged me tight and said, 'All I have of Dad now are his memories and photos in frames. I wanted to tell him while he was alive that I loved you and wanted to get married to you. But God took him away from me before I could tell him that.'

And then she recounted painfully all that had transpired following her father's demise.

'After three days of Dad's death, we received a letter from the bank. It was a notice regarding our loan payment. We had defaulted on the payment and so the bank officials had come for recovery. The amount was a considerable one for us. We all were worried about the payment. Finally, after a lot of discussion Mom called Dilip Uncle and asked him to come home. Dilip Uncle was Dad's closest friend and had been with us through thick and thin. Uncle was a part of our family. He came home the next evening on Mom's request.'

Riya recounted every word of their conversation.

'Dilip Uncle asked us the last date given by the bank for repaying the loan. I was sitting beside my Mom with a worried expression on my face. Mom told him that the last date was a lot closer than we expected it to be. He suggested that since the bank officials were on our head, he would pay the loan on our behalf and we could pay him back later when we had the money. It was such a sweet gesture on his part. We felt bad to take help from him, but we were left with no other option. He told us that Dad was a dear friend of his, almost like a brother. Uncle said that it would be his pleasure if he could help our family in any way possible.'

I was listening intently to every word Riya was saying.

'Mom and I both cried and thanked him for his generosity. He was no less than an angel for us. He made the loan payment and did not ask us even once in that by when we would repay it. If he had not helped us at that moment, situation, I don't know what would have happened to us. For the next few days, Dilip Uncle became a regular visitor to our house, visiting to check on our general health. Sometimes Dilip Uncle would even join us for dinner. He would tell my brother to study hard and that he would look after his graduation and would see to it that he gets admission in a reputed college. He told my brother not to think of anything else except studies and just work hard. His genuineness was clearly visible. He was indeed an angel sent by my father to look after us in his absence. I thanked God that night. He helped us in every possible way... He referred my brother's name to the trusty of a reputed college in Mumbai—Swami Vivekanad College. He did this even before my brother's final exams were over.'

'He sure sounds like an angel, Riya. Even blood relatives do not show so much concern as he did,' I chipped in.

'He sure was,' said Riya. 'Yesterday night, I told Dilip Uncle and Mom that I would join office from today. Dilip Uncle told me that there was no urgency unless I was feeling better. I told him that I can't take more leave and that I need to work for my team. I explained to him my working profile. He then said that he may have a better job for me as my profile sounded impressive. He said that I can work in his company and earn more than I am earning presently. He believes that with my experience, I deserve a better pay and a higher position. He even went a step ahead and said that if I had some qualms about joining his company, then he could refer me to a few other companies whose HR heads he knew well. I told him that I needed sometime to think. I couldn't take a quick decision but assured him that I would take the right decision, one which would be keeping in mind my family as well. He agreed and smiled. My Mom was overwhelmed by his giving nature and thanked God for all his kindness over us in absence of my Dad. That day I missed Dad a lot. I missed him more than ever before since his untimely death. Before leaving for office today, I just stared at his photo. I could feel his eyes telling me that we were in safe hands and that I should take the decision sensibly. Tears fell down from my eyes and I decided that I would agree to work under Dilip Uncle in his company.'

I had been so engrossed in her story that I failed to notice that night had fallen. 'Jaan, did I do anything wrong in accepting his offer? If you are against it, then I will rethink my decision,' Riya cried on my shoulders.

'No, my sweetheart, you can never be wrong. My love can never be wrong. If I had been in your place, I would have done the same thing. I am so thankful to Dilip Uncle who managed to help you in this time of crisis despite having his own family to take care of. If he is giving you a better position and salary in his company, then it would be foolish of you not to take him up on his offer. You deserve it. You have a much better profile than I do. Go ahead. Don't think over it again.'

I hugged her tightly. I didn't want to let her go from my arms. I was happy to see her progress in life.

As the days passed, Riya's financial condition improved considerably. We were all thankful to Dilip Uncle who gave her a much better job and also helped her brother excel in studies besides giving moral support to her Mom. I wanted to meet Dilip Uncle and thank him personally for his kindness. But I was aware that it was not my place to do so.

The confidence in Riya's body language, the glow on her face, and the sweet smile gradually returned. As days passed, Riya slowly managed to move on and accept the fact that her Dad won't come back to them. She knew she had to prove to him that his daughter could hold the family together even though he wasn't with them anymore.

One evening, Riya's family and Dilip Uncle's family decided to go for dinner together. Riya requested me to join them as I had told her once that I wanted to meet Dilip Uncle and see for myself their saviour. She told me she had convinced her Mom saying that I just wanted to meet her Uncle and that there was no hidden agenda behind it. I agreed to come at the decided venue.

I got into a nice suit and left my home. Riya had told me that they would be assembling at Shabri restaurant. I had mixed feelings and did not know how I would react when Riya would introduce me to Dilip Uncle. I stood outside the restaurant and reserved the table for us. Soon all of them arrived. I could single out Dilip Uncle from far itself. He was immaculately dressed in a black suit with a matching bow tie. He seemed to be a big executive of some company. As they came near, I sensed Riya's Mom was not happy to see me there. It was not because she didn't like me, but because I was an outsider for them. Riya introduced me to Dilip Uncle's family as a very good friend of hers and we shared greetings. He casually asked Riya whether we were just friends or seeing each other. Riya laughed and changed the topic. Dilip Uncle was just pulling her leg. We went inside and Riya signalled to me asking me to behave like a sophisticated person. I smiled at her.

'Where are you working, Aditya?' Dilip Uncle asked me while his son and wife looked at me.

'I am working in SGS in Malad.' I kept it short. He nodded and smiled.

Riya introduced me to Dilip Uncle's son Nikhil who worked as the General Manager in Dilip Uncle's company. We smiled at each other and exchanged a few pleasantries. Dilip Uncle asked Riya and her brother questions about their office and studies respectively until the food came. After having dinner, each of us ordered a sweet dish.

'What are your future plans, Riya?' Dilip Uncle asked.

'I just want to get settled and take care of my family. My family is my first priority as of now,' she answered.

'I just want to say something to all of you. It's just how I feel. No hard feelings,' he ventured, 'Actually, hmm... I don't know how to say this, but I have been looking for a girl for Nikhil. I asked him if he had someone in mind but he said no. I have been thinking about you for quite some time, Riya. You are a nice girl and understand your responsibilities; you will be perfect for Nikhil. I am not imposing my decision on you. It's just a suggestion.'

I swallowed with difficulty the spoonful of dessert. My head spun round. *What the fuck! What is he saying? Have I been consuming alchohol all this while? This is crazy.*

I looked at Nikhil. He seemed equally shocked at the announcement but managed a weak smile. I wanted to kill him at that moment. Everything happened in a fraction of second. Riya didn't utter a word nor did her Mom. I thought that I had lost her but she held my hands under the table to assure me that she was mine. I looked at her but she didn't even glance at me. She kept looking at her Mom and Dilip Uncle.

'I am not forcing you. You can definitely think it over. Don't take your decision in a hurry. I don't mind even if you decline my proposal,' said Dilip Uncle smiling at Riya's Mom.

The grip of Riya's hand made me feel that I was still her Mr Perfect. She knew how I felt at that moment. I should not have come for the dinner. It would not have hurt so much had Riya told me this over the phone. But I was sure she knew nothing of what was going on in Dilip Uncle's head all this time.

So that was why he had helped her out with all that money and a job and everything else. It was all part of his big plan to get Riya to marry his lame ass son! Few days back, I was waiting outside the registration office in my sherwani to get married to Riya. But circumstances changed, the tables turned. Today, I am sitting beside her and I am helpless.

Everyone finished their sweet dish and came out of the restaurant after the bill was paid, paid by who else, but the great, generous Uncle. I wanted to strangle him there and then.

I just kept looking at them as they drove away in their respective cars. Riya popped her head outside the car window to look at me till the time their car disappeared into darkness. I didn't move an inch. I wish we had gotten married that day.

I wanted to ask her if this was the way she wanted to be. She knew that without her I was so weak. Please… Don't go. People say I am strong but I need your hand. Don't leave me like this—so broken, so cold.

I looked at my cell and Riya's message popped up.

Don't worry, my jaan. I am yours and no one can separate us. I won't go away from you. I will talk to Mom about this.

I managed smile but the fear kept killing me. Was it the end? I don't want to end it this way. I wish I was the scriptwriter of my own life. I wished...

Can't Let Go of You

Riya and I met over a cup of coffee the next day. Her eyes seemed puffy and I could tell she had not slept very well after the disaster last night's dinner with Dilip Uncle turned out to be.

Taking a sip of her cappuccino, she said, 'After I reached home, I had a long, heated discussion with Mom. I told her that it was impossible for me to marry Nikhil as I had already devoted my life to you. But she did not take this very well. She kept on reminding me how Dilip Uncle had helped us out in crucial times and how we were obliged to him for having restored our lives back to normal.'

'But that is emotional blackmail, Riya,' I told her, trying to make her realize that her mother was trying to use her vulnerability to her advantage.

'I know that, Aditya. But she being my mother is right in her own way. All she is doing is looking out for us and making sure we are okay. I told her that even though I was grateful to Dilip Uncle for having helped us in times of need, it did not mean that I was going to repay him back for his kindness by pledging my own life in marriage to his son.'

Riya wiped away the tears from her eyes and continued, 'Mom would not hear a word of what I had to say and kept telling me that my priorities lied elsewhere. That angered me to no end. It's not that because I am in a relationship with you, I love my parents and my brother any less? I don't know where elders get such vague ideas from and why they turn up thinking we don't care for them enough when in a relationship.'

'Listen now, you don't need to cry over such a petty thing. You know I love you and nothing in this world can change that,' I said trying to comfort her.

She gave me a weak smile and thanked me softly, saying how she would be utterly lost without me. I chuckled and told her she would do just fine. After paying the bill, we left for our respective offices.

As the days passed, we saw lesser of each other as her Mom made sure to keep a close watch on her. We could not talk to each other as freely as we did before since her mother's overbearing shadow kept looming large over her head.

One evening, when her mother was away from the house, she gave me a call on the sly.

'Aditya, I have missed you so much. My mother has been trying her best to convince me to marry Nikhil. But I have put my foot down. The thing that hurts me the most is that she keeps on reminding me how I need to look out for my brother. Her twisted logic is that because Uncle has helped secure my brother admission in college, we are indebted to him forever. I so wished he would not have helped us in the first place. At least I would not be standing at such difficult crossroads today. Every act of his kindness is like a loan whose interest rate shoots up by the second.'

'I know that it is difficult for you to make a decision given the circumstances you are in,' I said to her on the phone.

'It's not just that, Adi. Every time I tell my Mom that I want to get married to you instead of Nikhil, she reminds me how you will not be able to fend for me, given that you are just starting out now in life, let alone support our family when the time will come. But money is not everything in life, right? There are other things that one can care about as well,' explained Riya.

'So what are your views on Nikhil? Do you find him good looking?' I said trying to ease the situation. But it did not help much.

'Please, Aditya. Looks is not the only thing that is desirable in another person. And why should I be bothered about his looks when I have eyes only for you? I love you, Aditya. I can't love anyone else. This never-ending saga seems like it is testing my love for you. On the one hand, I can't go against my family. There is no one to look after them, no one to care of them besides me. I have already lost my father. I can't afford to lose my mother as well. But on the other hand, I love you so deeply. Even the thought of parting from you is unimaginable,' said Riya.

'So why keep these thoughts if they cause you such pain? Just drive them away and think about how, very soon, we are going to be reconciled together,' I told her in an assured tone, even though our future together looked hazy at the moment.

'Why is it that most of the times, a girl chooses her lover over her parents? In most cases, she runs away from home and get settled without thinking once about the shame it will cause her parents. At this particular junction, I am facing the same dilemma. I feel so helpless, Aditya. I am burdened with so many responsibilities and no one can deal with it except me. I need to take a decision fast. I think Mom is back. I will give you a call tomorrow,' said Riya hurriedly and hung up the phone.

I reluctantly went to bed after our conversation was cut short by her mother's entry. But sleep evaded me. All through our conversation, Riya sounded a little lost to me. I kept wondering what decision she would eventually end up making. Will she decide to be with me or will she go with the decision made by her mother? I pushed the thoughts away from my mind and tried to get some sleep.

A Decision is Made

It was just another morning; I opened my eyes thinking about her when the alarm bell interrupted my dream. Reluctantly, I got up to get ready for office. However, the day had something entirely else in the store. I dropped the plan of going to office and started waiting anxiously for her phone. I picked the phone twice to call her but something stopped me. I took my bike to buy some roses. My ears were by then desperate to hear the ring tone that I had especially set for her. I was so desperate to hear Riya say that she had declined the proposal.

And finally, she called me.

We started talking. As usual, I gave her a morning kiss on the phone. She told me she wanted to meet me.

I reached the designated place before time. While waiting for her to come, I saw a card gallery nearby, and went in to buy something for her. After much deliberation, I finally settled for a small soft toy and some roses. I was getting impatient and was eagerly looking at each passing cab, thinking might be carrying her.

Ah! I caught her first glimpse after so many days. She was looking extremely beautiful. Her each step was bringing her nearer to me, making my breathing heavier and uneven.

And then I spotted her. She was walking towards me in a hurry. She smiled graciously and extended forward her hand to greet me. I found her gesture a bit odd. Usually we would kiss or hug, but she seemed to have her mind occupied on something altogether different. We sat in a restaurant and I ordered a few snacks for us. After the waiter had taken the order and left the two of us alone, she told me with a heavy voice that she had accepted the proposal and was ready to marry Nikhil.

I was not sure of how to react to that. Suddenly all my excitement was gutted. I couldn't believe what I was hearing.

'Are you insane? I understand your situation, but please cut the crap. This is utter nonsense. I am perfectly capable of supporting you financially. I would do whatever you want. Why are you doing this to me?' Even though I told her I was ready to take on her and her family's responsibility, both of us knew better. It would be impossible for me to look after her brother's education on my meagre salary. But I was ready to try. I would have done anything. I would have robbed a bank for all it was worth. As long as she was with me.

'Do you think any of this is easy for me? Do you think I can stop loving you? I love you and will always do,' she said hugging me tightly.

'Then please change your decision. I don't want you to take one wrong step and repent it all your life,' I said while holding her by her waist and kissing her neck. I gave her the roses and the soft toy I had bought for her earlier. She smiled and got up to leave. With a heavy heart, I waved her goodbye.

As I put my bike in gear, Mohit called me.

'Aadi, I hope you guys are coming one week before the marriage, right? I want you here this time and don't want any excuses. Sonam just called Riya and she has agreed to come. She said she will coordinate with you and leave for Chandigarh accordingly.'

'Sure, buddy. Finally, your marriage date is here. There is hardly any time left. Congrats!'

We chatted for a bit and hung up. I did not want to tell him all that was happening back in Mumbai. That would have unnecessarily upset him and I wanted him to enjoy his leftover bachelorhood days as much as he could. Riya and I decided to leave Mumbai for Chandigarh the following week.

It's the Season of Love

The wedding was supposed to take place in Chandigarh, Sonam's ancestral home. Even though Riya and I travelled together, not much was spoken along the way. I tried to convince Riya to reject the proposal, but she refused to say anything. While Mohit and Sonam's love story was on the right track, our love story was taking a different turn. We reached Chandigarh and Sonam's family car was there to escort us. On the way, we asked the driver about where the groom was lodged. He told us that Mohit was staying in a bungalow near Sonam's. I had informed Mohit that we would reach in a couple of hours. As our car entered the lawn, I saw that the house was decorated with lights of different colours and wedding flowers. It looked like a big, fat Punjabi wedding which is famous for its grandeur and opulence. Punjabis are known to pull all the stops when it comes to their weddings.

Mohit and Sonam were both waiting for us at the entrance. We got down from the car and congratulated them with a warm hug. I was amazed at how perfect everything looked. The entire lawn had been decorated with pink and orange silk cloths to form the ceiling canopy. It had a beautiful garden with creepers that had been coiled with lights. There were fresh flower centerpieces kept on each table with chairs that had been tied with a pretty pink bows. The house was beautifully set up for the function.

'So this is what heaven looks like. This is really a grand wedding.' I looked at Sonam and she smiled back.

'Thanks a lot. It needed a lot of hard work and time,' said Sonam.

'You've done an excellent job, Sonam,' added Riya.

'We are extremely sorry for your loss. I told Mohit that we should postpone our engagement date but you wouldn't agree. I hope everything is alright now.' Sonam held Riya's hand as we walked.

'I know, Aditya told me about it. Your celebrations should not get hindered by anything, that's what I thought,' Riya tried to smile.

Sonam's parents saw us coming and they came out to greet us. It is rare that one meets wealthy people who are also down-to-earth at the same time. Sonam sure was lucky to have parents like them.

Sonam's parents welcomed us by putting a garland around both our necks. Everything seemed planned to perfection.

'Sonam, tell your Dad to sponsor Riya and my wedding too. Please,' I jokingly whispered to her.

'Shut up, Aadi!' she pinched me.

We kept our bags in one of the rooms and took a nap for a few hours. Sonam and Mohit were still not aware of the critical condition of our relationship. I wanted to tell them but it was not the appropriate time. Riya would have killed me if I would have done such thing, especially when their wedding day was hardly a few days away.

'Aditya, get ready for the sangeet ceremony. The function is about to start in the lawn. Let's go,' Riya came and told me.

She took no time to mix with Sonam's family and relatives and actively participated in all the work. She went to get Sonam who was getting ready in her room for the ceremony. I heard a few close relatives from Mohit's side were also called for the function. I was wearing a black kurta while Riya had chosen to wear a pink kurti with a yellow patiala salwar, just right for the occassion. The ceremony began and some aunties started singing songs and playing the dholki.

Sonam's family teased Mohit's family members who were present in the ceremony, through songs. All in good jest, of course, but they took care not to get carried away. Everyone danced to the tune of bhangra songs.

Sonam's Dad sang a song for Sonam's Mom in front of the entire family.

Raat kali, ek khwaab me aayi aur gale ka haar hui...
It was her Mom's turn then who sang;
Haal kaisa hai janab ka, kya khayal hai aapka,
Tum toh machal gaye oh oh oh
Yuhi phisal gaye ha ha ha
I was having a time. The next song was sung by Sonam's Dad.
Gore rang pe na itna khumaar kar, gora rang to din me dhal jaayenga....
Mein shama hu, tu hai parwana... Mujhse pehle tu jal jaayega....
Mohit came and this time it was Riya's turn. I almost fell down on the floor for this one.
Raam chandra keh gaye siya se... hans chugega daana dunaka, kauva moti khaayega....
The war went on....

When we came to the end of fantastic sangeet ceremony, everyone became emotional as Sonam's parents hugged her and cried. It brought tears to my eyes too. I visualized my sister at that moment.

We had a royal feast after the ceremony and went to sleep. The fun we had all day brought a smile to my face. I wanted to have these very moments with Riya, but I didn't know what the future held for us.

I wished their marriage brought them all the happiness they so rightly deserved. I wished for Sonam that life grant her all the patience, tolerance, and understanding to live with Mohit.

May they always be with each other till the end of time.
If they have quarrels that push them apart, may they have
the good sense enough to take the first step back.

I wanted to pour my heart out in front of Mohit. I
wanted to tell him what had been going on with Riya
and me since the past few days. I finally decided to tell
him before the mehendi function.

Mehendi was the last major function before the
wedding. Mehendiwallis had been called to both their
places to apply henna on the bride's hands and feet all
the relatives. A basket containing bindis and bangles was
handed around for girls to choose ones that matched
the outfits they planned on wearing to the wedding.

I saw my opportunity once everyone got busy applying
mehendi and went straight to Mohit's room. He was
shocked to see me standing there as he expected me to
be at the mehendi function.

'Mohit, I need to discuss something serious with
you.' I sat down on the bed.

'What happened, any problem with Riya? Did you
fight again?' he asked curiously.

'No. Why would we fight? That too during these
days when she needs me the most! This is something
extremely serious,' I said.

I told him everything that had happened in the last few days. I told him about Nikhil. I told him about Riya's decision to marry him.

'What the fuck are you talking about?' Mohit raised his eyebrows. 'Riya and Nikhil, yuck… That sounds ridiculous. Riya only looks good when she is with you. I promise you that before my marriage, I will talk with her once,' Mohit added.

It made me feel much better. All I could do was to hope for good things to happen. I went back to the mehendi ceremony where Riya was singing a song as she held Sonam from the back.

Mehendi hai rachne waali, haathon me gehri laali….
I smiled looking at Riya. She seemed to be having a good time. But I knew that beneath her calm façade, she was hiding her sorrows and worries. I went and sat close to her. I saw her hands. She had written her name and mine with mehendi on her left hand. It brought a big smile on my face. I wanted to kiss her hard, but I couldn't because there were so many people around us.

'I love you.' She simply smiled and held my hand with the other hand on which she was yet to apply mehendi.

Sonam's mehendi was looking extremely beautiful. It was up to her elbows and looked so intricate and delicate on her. She showed me both her hands. The happiness and satisfaction of getting married to a person you love was visible in her eyes… I stared at Riya. I stared at her mehendi in silence.

I cannot promise never to be angry; I cannot promise always to be kind. You know what you are taking on, my darling. It's only at the start that love is blind and yet I'm still the one you want to be with. You're the one for me. I'm sure. You are my closest friend, my favourite person, my love, and the wife I've waited for. I cannot promise that I deserve you. From this day on, I hope to pass that test. I love you and I want to make you happy. I promise I would do my very best.

The maaiyan of the bride starts three days before the wedding, which means she is then not supposed to leave the house until the big day. These days are meant for complete relaxation. She is not even supposed to meet the groom. As if Mohit could stay away! Or for that matter, even Sonam!

'Has nervousness kicked in already? Poor you, now you can't meet Mohit till the wedding day. So tell me frankly, are you nervous?', I asked Sonam.

'Of course, I am. Any girl would be in my place. Even Riya will get nervous during your marriage,' she said. I was zapped.

Regaining my composure, I continued, 'Why are you nervous?'

'I will be leaving my parents' house and going into a family that is completely unknown to me, except for Mohit. But his presence doesn't count. So sure, I am nervous.'

'Oh, that is the case. I thought…'

'What did you think? Speak up!' She was eager to know.

'I thought you were nervous about your wedding night,' I snickered and ran away.

Wedding Bells are Ringing

Finally, the wedding day arrived!

The day, which holds utmost importance in a person's life. It can either bring you immense amount of happiness or completely ruin your life. All of us has been waiting for this day. That morning seemed different from all the previous mornings.

Marriage is a relationship or a responsibility which two people accept in their life. It is about standing together and facing the world. It is never taking the other for granted; the courtship should not end with the honeymoon, it should continue through the years. It is remembering to say 'I love you' at least once a day. It is never going to sleep angry. It is doing things for each other, not in the attitude of duty or sacrifice, but in the spirit of joy. It is establishing a relationship in which the independence is equal, dependence is mutual and the obligation is reciprocal. It is not only 'marrying' the right partner, it is 'being' the right partner.

Mohit had found the right partner for himself in Riya. It started with a casual meeting and today they were about to take the sacred vows together. Special attention was paid to include a generous dose of the colour red in the wedding. The red curtains and red covers added the essence of romance to the day. The red candles, the red lamps, and even the red vases gave it a romantic feel.

The haldi ceremony was about to begin. The friends and family proceeded to dip their fingers in a bowl containing the haldi paste and smeared it all over Mohit and Sonam! The purpose was to make their skin glow for the special day.

Not even an inch of their bodies was spared. We made sure that every inch of Mohit's face, neck, arms, chest, legs, and feet was covered. Rest of the parts we left clothed. We spared Mohit that much.

'Beta, wait till your marriage!' Mohit exclaimed.

'Oh really, should I apply a thick paste on your ...' I laughed.

He went red faced and didn't say anything.

After sometime, Mohit and Sonam had an orange glow to their bodies, which looked superb.

'Sonam, you have got the perfect glow before the wedding,' said Riya with excitement.

'She is getting ready for tonight,' Mohit piped in. Sonam took a thick paste of haldi and applied it all over his hair and face to tease him. They looked so cute together.

After the haldi ceremony, Mohit and Sonam went to bathe the to wash off all the paste. Everyone else was busy getting ready for the chuda ceremony. This was my favourite part of Punjabi weddings. I looked the most excited to witness it. The priest started performing the puja and Sonam's maternal Uncle made her wear a set of chuda after washing it in milk. The bangles are considered a symbol of love. Red and silver, with the couples' names carved on it. I glanced at Riya and she too stared at me. We shared a naughty smile as we both imagined the same thing.

Sonam's Uncle had brought some gifts for her parents. To wish Sonam with all the blessings, her cousins and friends tied kaleeras, which were silver plated dangling bangles and had red silk threads on with them.

'Sonam, if I had known that you would look so beautiful on your wedding day, I would have proposed to you before Mohit,' I said lightheartedly and Riya immediately reacted to it with a tight punch on my back.

After the chuda ceremony, some of the family broke into spontaneous bhangra dance!

The Punjabis are known for their grand weddings. A Punjabi wedding is a joyful and an extravagant affair, comprising of many colourful customs and rituals which bring together relatives and friends alike. They add to the excitement and happiness.

At last, the two couples were to tie the knot in the next few hours. After a long journey of love, they were one step closer to a happy life together. We were still far behind them. We were still stuck with the hurdles in our way.

It was time for Mohit to sit on the ghodi or the traditional wedding horse and take the baraat to Sonam's bungalow. The baraat started off with a display of fireworks. It was also accompanied by the rhythm of the dhol. We danced as if we were drunk. A proper baraat dance! Two drummers from Gujarat announced the arrival of the groom outside Sonam's bungalow in a stately style. After the baraat arrived, the milni ceremony was carried out. Mohit's father embraced Sonam's father quiting of and this was followed by the rest of the family members. It was symbolic of the unification of the two families.

Sonam looked drop dead gorgeous as she walked towards the mandap of the wedding. Her red and maroon lehenga had heavy work all over it. She had taken her dupatta over her head, which made her look no less than a princess. She made for a perfect bride! Even her jewellery and heels matched her outfit.

Walking beside her was Riya who looked lovely. She was wearing a blue silk sari that showed off her slim figure.

Both Mohit and Sonam came towards the centre and big garlands were to them, which they handed exchanged. The pundit started with his chants and asked both of them to get up and wak around the sacred fire seven times. The pheres began and Riya and I looked at each other. Long back, we too had taken the seven promises.

'You remember the promises we took?' I asked her.

She nodded.

As Mohit and Sonam took the first of the seven phere, I whispered in Riya's ear, 'Promise one. We will always be together.'

She stared at me while the grip on my hand tightened.

'Promise three. We will not let our love fade.' I made Riya realize that she had once promised never to let go of me. She didn't say anything but looked away from me towards the mandap. I slowly wiped tear from my eye. Maybe, it had to end!

The pheres got over and Sonam's Dad proceeded with her kanyadaan.

I went close to Riya and saw that she was silently crying. I brought her close to me and asked her the reason.

'Who will come forward for my kanyadaan? Whenever I get married, I know Dad that you will be praying for me from there.' She pointed towards the sky.

'Jaan, please don't think like this. We are all with you. We would never let you feel the absence of your Dad in your life. We all love you,' I consoled her.

'I know you all love me. However, my Dad holds a special place in my heart. I once dreamed about getting married. I once dreamed about my Dad sitting beside me for my kanyadaan and giving me a warm farewell. This can never turn into reality. I miss my Dad,' she cried some more.

I tried to wipe her tears but she was inconsolable. It was difficult to make things okay again. It was next to impossible to fill the place of her Dad. It broke me to see her so sad.

It was time for Sonam to leave her family behind, leave behind the childhood memories related to her house. Everyone from Sonam's family had tears in their eyes.

Sonam went and hugged her father. They both had tears in their eyes. Mohit went ahead and touched her parents' feet, assuring them that he would always take care of her.

Sonam hugged her Mom for the final time before leaving. They both just looked at each other and held each other's hands.

She then turned towards Riya and me and said, 'Aditya, as you are well aware, Riya suffered a big loss a few days back. Please take care of her always and never let her out of your sight. And by the time Mohit and I come back from our honeymoon, we hope to hear the good news that you are getting married next.'

Mohit had not told her anything. While departing, she threw puffed rice over her head, another ritual indicating she was leaving behind good wishes for her parents. Finally, she sped away to her new life.

'Jaan, we are staying here for one more day. I need to spend some time with you. I want to live my whole life in one day with you. I want to hold your hand and roam around the city. I want to hug you where no one can see us. I want to kiss you where no one can point at us. I want to…' said Riya after settling down in her room.

'Sure, sweetheart. I would love to be with you forever. I still want to hold you tight in my arms and never let you go. The feeling of being alone without you by my side kills me,' I said. I wondered whether our end was closer, keeping my fingers crossed.

We had decided to stay in Chandigarh for one more day. Riya wanted to spend a day with me alone. We stayed in Sonam's house that night. I decided to plan something special for Riya for the following day. We wanted to live for one more day. We wanted to love each other for one more day.

The meaning of love is not to be confused with some sentimental outpouring. Love is something much more than an emotional release. Love is the most durable power in the world. Love is not breathlessness, it is not excitement, and it is not the declaration of promises of eternal passion. Love itself is what is left over when being in love has burned away.

Unrequited Promises

After the tiring festivities of the day before, I woke up to a fresh morning in Punjab. We had planned to spend a day with each other. I wanted to make this day memorable for her. I wanted her to remember our college days where I used to give her surprises and pamper her a lot. I wanted her to free her mind from tension and just enjoy the moment with me. I brought some gifts for her from a nearby gift shop. I had asked Sonam certain places where we could hang out and spend some time together.

'Where are we going?' she asked me and held my hand as we walked.

'Rose garden. Bachha, get ready for some surprises,' I smiled.

She blushed and held my hands tightly. She planted a kiss on my cheek as we walked towards Hotel Shivalik View. We hopped into a double-decker bus. We took our seats and as she tried to open her purse, I removed a rose from my pocket.

'A rose for the lady!' I said and kissed her hand.

'You are the best,' she said and kept her head on my

shoulder. I felt my shoulder getting wet. I looked down and saw the tears in Riya's eyes.

'Don't cry, jaan. I love you and will always support you. Don't start this beautiful day with tears in your eyes. You know that I hate it when girls cry. If you cry, your eyeliner will get smudged,' I teased. The trick worked and Riya was soon her jovial self again.

We reached Rose Garden after sometime. There were roses of all colours, beautiful trees flowing with colourful blossoms, numerous other flowering plants. Several pathways wind in around the gardens. There were benches to sit in while many people sat on the grass. It was romantic. We roamed around for some time and saw the beautiful fountain, which added to the beauty and romance of the garden. We sat in one corner of the garden. Riya sat beside me and leaned into me. I took out a letter from my bag and kept it on her lap. It reminded me of my early days with Riya. She was flattered seeing the letter on her lap. Without opening it, she hugged me and kissed my neck. Her eyes were filled with tears. I let her read the letter.

My sweetheart,

Whenever I see a new morning, I call out your name, but these days, it's different. These days, love and sadness have become my perennial fear. You are the only love of my life. Please don't push me away like you don't care. I try to shout at you to be with me, but only the morning breeze hears me. Don't you know that I need you beside me? Don't ever stop thinking of me. Don't stop caring.

Have faith in me as I have in you. I can only hope that this is just a minor setback, but deep down, I know it's the end. I know the last few years of our relationship will be forgotten. Nevertheless, I won't let this happen. Not this time for sure. I hate that I can't go a day without having you on my mind. I'm lost. You are everything to me and losing you would be the worst pain I could endure. I pray every day and hope that you be with me forever. Just please. Please don't leave me. I understand you have priorities in your life and I am proud of it. I am proud that you value your family and care for them. As children are lucky to get parents, who value their thoughts, even your parents are lucky to have someone like you to take care of them. I would never suggest you to go against your family and live with me. I know your family needs you more than I do. However, I need you no less than them. I assure you that we can be happy and take care of your family. Please trust me, sweetheart. For the last time, have blind faith in me!

She closed her eyes after reading the letter and looked at me with tearful eyes.

'Why do you do this? Why do you make me feel that no one can take your place? Why do you make me realize that you are the only one perfect companion for me? Every time you do this, I am left speechless,' she said kissing me on my lips.

I could feel her pain at that moment. Sometimes we are so helpless, yet we want to give our best. We remained in the same position for a few minutes and then stared at each other for a long time after that. The pain of separation was evident. The pain of loneliness approaching us was imminent. I wanted to shout out loud 'no one will love you more than me'.

We decided to return after grabbing a quick bite at the nearby reataurant.

We were returning by the bus when Mohit called us. He had left for Dalhousie in the morning.

'Hey Aadi, this place is fucking romantic. I am missing our office trip days when we had so much fun together. Get married soon and we will come back to this place again,' he said and hung up. I had the phone on loudspeaker.

We both looked at each other. Silence filled the air. We could sense each other's thoughts. I remembered the night Riya wore her black dress and we made love in the hotel room. How I rolled strawberries all over her and kissed her from head to toe. It had been such a romantic night.

'I don't want to go away from you. This time I can't take it.' I couldn't control my tears. She brought me near her and played with my hair. She didn't speak a word. We reached Rock Garden. It was huge and very well lay out. It was well maintained and the odd shapes and waste materials were used in an amazing way to make various figures. There was a small waterfall in the garden and other beautiful things to see. There were some funny mirrors too. We went near the waterfall and settled down. I started questioning Riya.

'What do you love about me?' I asked, breaking the silence.

'I love your simplicity, I love the way you pamper me. I love your smile and everything about you makes me fall for you. Why are you asking me like this?' she smiled.

'To make you realize that you love me and can't live without me,' I said.

She turned her face around and kept quite. I handed her a Ganesha idol packed in a gift wrapper and told her to unwrap it. She loved the idol and made a sweet face looking at it.

She hugged me and said 'so sweet of you'.

I smiled and played with her hair. Her face glittered when she saw that idol. I handed her one more letter. She stared at me and then started reading.

Why do you no longer want me? I don't know what to say. I thought our relationship was perfect, why didn't you think of me even once? I know we could have fixed the problem. Why can't you give me a chance? Why? If you say you love me and that you can't live without me, why can we not give this another try? My heart feels empty and hollow. I thought this time no one could separate us. I don't want to lose you forever. Don't you remember our romantic nights in Manali, where we cuddled with each other, and made sweet love until day break? I think we broke the flower vase too that night. On top of that, I remember very well that it was your idea. How can you forget the chuda you bought just because it was my wish? Our name carved over it, I thought Aditya and Riya couldn't be separated. They are one. Why do you want to change that? I would take care of your family. I know your family is your utmost priority and it has to be. However, don't leave me all alone.

This time, she cried like a small baby. I tried to calm her down and wipe her tears, but failed. Everything was a mess.

After spending the entire day together, we were ready to pack our bags and leave for Mumbai.

When we arrived at the Mumbai airport, neither of us wanted to leave for home, not knowing what the future held for us.

'We will go home tomorrow. Let's go to some resort till then,' said Riya.

We boarded a taxi and cruised our way towards Pali Chowk road. We decided to stay in Pali Beach Resort for the night and then leave for our respective houses the next day. As there was less traffic on the roads at night, we reached within an hour's time. The resort was built beautifully and faced the majestic Arabian Sea.

We had booked an air-conditioned room for our stay. Soon, as we both were tired, we drifted off to sleep.

I didn't realize when the clock struck ten in the morning. I just opened my eyes lying on the bed. Riya

was in front of the dressing table. I was tired after the
hectic journey and my body ached. I didn't get up from
the bed. Riya went out of the room and came back in
some time. I took a bath until she came back.

When she came back, she told me to get ready fast,
saying she had a surprise waiting for me. I got ready and
asked her what it is. She went out and told me to wait.
I was excited and nervous at the same time.

She came inside with a trolley. On it was three-tiered
cake in the colours of white, red and silver, with little
cherubs, roses, and hearts on it.

I read the letters that were beautifully carved in red on
the cake.

HAPPY PROPOSAL DAY MY LOVE!

And here I was thinking that she had forgotten the
first time we met!

She handed me a knife and told me to cut the cake.
I cut the cake which had a velvet covering. I took the
first piece and smeared it all over her face.

'No… I will kill you,' she shouted trying to open
her eyes.

'Now tell me sweetheart, which colours do you like
the most on this cake?' I asked her putting some more
cake on her face.

'Shut up, Aadi. I can barely see and you are asking
me my favourite colour?'

'Why do you want to take the trouble of washing
your face when I am right here beside you?' I said.

She lowered her voice and said, 'What do you mean?' Her eyes were still closed.

'I mean tell me your favourite colour, jaan.' I went close to her.

'Red!'

I bent down to her and licked all the red cream off her face. Then I went ahead and licked the white cream too. She shyly pushed me away. Then I lifted her in my arms and carried her to the bed. And then we made love, with me licking the cake from all over her face and Riya moaning in response.

Exhausted, we lay down on the bed holding each other. We looked into each other's eyes and she said she had something more to show me.

'What?' I asked her with enthusiasm.

She wrapped the bed sheet around her body to cover herself and walked towards the dressing table. She opened the drawer and removed a gift wrapped in red coloured paper. It seemed like a cloth or a piece of paper. I was curious to open it. She made me promise that I won't get angry after seeing it. I promised her the same. I unwrapped the cover to see a folded paper. It was a letter.

I know how it feels to be in your position. I know how it feels to be alone. However, if you would look carefully at me, I am trying my best to protect our relationship. I want to be with you forever. You mean a lot to me. You have shown me what love is and what it feels like to be loved. You are the beat of my heart, the soul in my body; because without you I am nothing. You are the person I know I can turn to when I need help, you are the person I look at when I needed to smile, and you are the person I went to when I need a hug. When I am away, it is as if I have left my soul behind. You have shown me how to live and you have shown me how to be truly happy. I want you to know that every time I smile, you have put it there. You make me smile when others can't; you make me feel warm when I am cold. You have shown me so much love and so much more. I want you to know how much you mean to me. You are my whole world and I love you with all my heart. You are my happiness. Tomorrow if I am not with you, please forgive me. I can't predict our future but for this moment, I am yours. I can't assure the happy end to our love story but for this moment, I want to spend happy moments with you. I can never forget the days we spent together, I can never forget your touch, and I hope you remember me and be happy always. I would try my best to be with you. I would fight with the world until my hand reaches someone else's hand. Trust me! No matter with who I am, my love for you can never die. You will be my Aadi, you will be my jaan, and you will be my bachha forever. No one can steal that right from me. Not even you. I love you, darling!

I don't know what our future was going to be but I loved her. I loved her honesty, I loved her simplicity, I loved her beauty, and I loved everything about her!

We just looked at each other through the rest of our time at the hotel without speaking a word.

Love is a Losing Game

It had been two days since our arrival in Mumbai. I had not seen Riya after our little night together in that resort, nor had we talked on the phone.

I had come back from office and was about to take a bath, when I got a message on my cell phone.

I opened the message inbox to see an unread message from Riya!

I know you were waiting for my message. I wanted to tell you so many things that day, but I couldn't find the courage to do so. I wanted to tell you that I may not be with you but the truth is I may not forget you my entire life. You have made a deep impact on me. The evening, which we spent together yesterday, has left me in a state of turmoil. Are you angry at me? Whenever you feel alone, just close your eyes and think of me. My heart is broken but I can't blame you. You took each broken piece of my heart and put it together like a puzzle. My heart was missing that piece during the times he stayed apart, but after you came back into my life, the last piece was placed that everything seemed perfect. It was then I realized that I can't live without you. I am writing this message lying on the same bed where you and I slept together and shared the best moments of our lives. You will always remain an integral part of me. If I am not with you, which I hope won't be the case; never let your tears fall down. I love you and will always love you. I wish I wouldn't be separated from you. When love is pure, love is pain. When love is true, love is sacrifice. Not everyone gets a chance to experience it.

Riya's message was the last jab to my heart. It led to my complete emotional breakdown in me. I still had a firm trust that our relationship would work. I trusted her and the decisions she made.

I messaged her back.

I trust you. I trust your love. I know it can't get over like this. Our moments of love, our fights, our jokes, our falling tears—they can't end so easily. We tore down all the walls between us, endured a lot of pain, hurt, and torture just to stay with each other. It can't get over so easily. Without your kisses, I just can't breathe anymore. I trust your judgement. I know that you value relations and won't make any wrong decisions in life. I accept your decision, whatever it maybe. All I know is we can never stay away from each other. Now don't think much and take rest. We both are tired and need some sleep. I will take a bath and then go to sleep. My shift timings are the same, from 9.30 am in the morning. Oh, by the way, I forgot to ask, would you want to join me in the shower? :D Lolz… Muaahhh!! Love you!!

After taking a bath, I slept, as I had to get up early for work. I checked my cell phone before sleeping but

Riya hadn't replied. *She must be tired and must have slept early*, I thought resting my head on the pillow.

I reached office in the morning to be greeted by a grumpy manager who told me to do over time because of my uninformed leaves and poor performance. I had no excuses left. I missed Mohit a lot that day. If he would have been present, he would have manipulated my attendance sheet and performances and then submitted it to the manager. Now I woud have to do dual shifts back to back. I wanted to meet Riya after my shift, but my manager made it impossible for me. It was hardly two hours into my work and I was already feeling sleepy. I grabbed a coffee in the hope of keeping awake and checked my cell phone. Still there was no response from Riya. She must be sleeping. Her second shift started at three in the afternoon. I got back to the work desk.

I opened my MS Outlook messenger to check my emails. I had an email from the HR department. I had won a performance award for my scores two months back. I understood why my manager had shouted at me in the morning and told me to improve my performance. It was because there had been a drastic downfall in my scores and he was worried about that. I was so glad to see that mail. I wished I could have maintained the scores for which I won the award. I was so excited that I left my desk and called Riya from the cafeteria. I wanted to tell her about it. She would be more excited than even me. The phone rang, but she didn't pick up. I messaged her about the award and continued my work. I wanted to talk with her.

After a long day in office, even a long night, I finished my shift hours. It was early morning when I left office and reached home. I tried calling Riya but still she didn't take my calls. I thought she might have slept. I too was tired after a hectic day at the office and dozed off in no time.

'Aditya, get up, you have been sleeping for so long. Let's have dinner,' my Mom shouted at me and I woke up.

I saw the clock. It was eight in the evening. I got up and searched for my mobile. I checked for any messages or calls from Riya. Still the home screen was blank. No messages and no missed calls. Where was she? I had my dinner in silence. I kept my mobile on the table and went to the washroom. Suddenly, the phone rang. I ran towards the table and saw my mobile.

It was an unknown number. I picked the call immediately.

'Hello, is it Riya?' My voice betrayed my desperation.

'Good evening sir, we are calling from Vodafone. Your phone number has been selected for a special offer. Are you interested?'

My frustration reached its peak. I wanted to fire that customer care executive but I was not in a mood to argue or fight with Vodafone agents. I disconnected the call. I dialled Riya's number again. She didn't respond.

Fuckk! This is absolute crap! This is unbelievable. Long back, I had seen a dream. Long back, I had a nightmare where Riya was hospitalized. Even then a Vodafone customer care executive had called me from an unknown number. This sent a chill down my spine. *How could this be happening now? Can dreams come true?*

I thought for a moment about where she could be and decided to go to her home in Navi Mumbai. I took my bike keys and left home. I tried to think positive while riding the bike. I consoled myself by thinking that nothing happened. I consoled my mind by thinking that dreams like these can't come true. This happens only in Bollywood movies. It can't happen with me in real life. However, the fact was that Bollywood movies are inspired from real life characters. Still, I tried to keep my calm. I reached her apartment with a tensed mind. I saw that her scooty was missing. Just like I had witnessed in the dream. I went upstairs but no one opened the door. I searched for her scooty in the entire complex. I called her number again. Still no one responded.

I wanted to kill myself right away. My dream was playing out scene by scene right in front of my very eyes! I tried to remember what happened next in my dream. Yes, I had gone to the hospital. I decided to look for her scooty outside the hospital. On reaching the hospital, I tried to find her scooty everywhere in the parking lot but couldn't locate it. I still gave another look around but it wasn't there. I wanted to remove this doubt from my mind, so I entered the hospital and went straight to the receptionist's desk.

'Is there any patient by the name of Riya?' I asked her.

She opened the register and started searching for the name. I was almost in tears by that time. I kept my fingers crossed and just closed my eyes for a moment. Tears rolled down my eyes.

'No. I am sorry. There is no one by this name,' she replied.

'Can you check again, please?' I asked her. I remembered my dream. She replied with the same answer. I finally relaxed. My doubt was cleared. The dream was just a dream. I finally regained my senses and walked out of the hospital. I started my bike and went to her apartment again. I parked my bike outside and called her. Still no response. I decided to go upstairs.

On reaching her doorstep, I found that the door was locked. I sat on the steps as my tears fell on the floor.

I realized I had lost her forever. I realized that I was not going to see her anymore. *I wished for it to be a dream so that you could come and wake me up with a sweet kiss.*

I called Sameer and told him to reach Riya's apartment as soon as possible. I called Sonam too and asked her to get in touch with Riya, explaining to her how Riya had not been taking my calls and how the door to her apartment was locked, with no sign of its occupants anywhere. 'Sonam, please call Riya. I tried searching for her everywhere from past two hours. Even her door is locked.

'Don't panic. Just relax. She might have messaged you, but due to some network problem, the message may not have reached. Let me call her,' said Sonam and kept the phone down. Mohit was with her.

I was all alone sitting on the steps thinking of her last message to me. It had been a while since our last day together, but to me, it seemed like years had passed. I never thought that the end would come so soon. *I wanted you to stay with me forever, but you have left me in a lurch. You missed the words I Love You! I tried to say it loud, screaming, so you could hear it. Everybody heard me except you. My dreams now lay shattered. The sweet jingle of your bangles will forever remain a dream!*

After what seemed like an eternity, Sonam called me.

'Aadi, she is not responding to my calls. I called her several times. Both Mohit and I have been calling her non-stop since the time you told us what had happened. If she calls back, I will immediately let you know. We are coming this week. So please don't worry,' she said and kept the phone.

Sameer had reached by that time. He asked me straight off, 'Did you try calling on her Mom's cell? Did you try calling anywhere else?'

'I tried calling each and everyone through whom I could come to know anything about Riya. No one seemed to know anything. I tried her Mom's cell too. It was fucking switched off. I think I have lost her forever,' I cried.

'Be positive, yaar. Keep your hopes up. You know she loves you more than anything in the world, don't you?' Sameer tried explaining to me.

'How can I keep calm when I know that I have lost my love and may never get to see her again?' I howled in front of Sameer.

Our relationship was meant to be everlasting. It was meant to be one of those successful love stories which would have a happy ending. We could have told our children about our love story. Now, after two years, time seemed to have come to a standstill. The sand clock had dropped on the floor and broken. It happened just when I was overturning it so that it never stops. *I was thinking of you and forgot to be careful. I tried to clue the pieces together again, but it didn't work. Everything is broken. I'm broken. The kisses are gone. The smile is now only a memory. You have left me forever; your love is gone. You left me alone, without asking me, without thinking about what I wanted. If I could only see you once more, if I could feel those lips one more time… But I know it won't happen.*

Sameer left after making me promise that I won't act rashly and think with a calm mind about what my next course of should be action. The next day when my Mom was reading the newspaper, I sat beside her and kept my head on her lap. She stopped reading and looked at me. She knew something was wrong. I began to weep. I told her everything that had happened. She kept the newspaper aside and stroked my hair gently.

'Aditya, you love her very much, right?'

My answer was an obvious yes. It had to be! Not a single doubt about it.

'If you don't mind, can I tell you one thing? Don't overreact, alright? Just listen to me carefully and then think over it,' said Mom.

I agreed and let her speak.

'I don't know much about Riya. My impression of her is drawn from all that you have told me about her in the past few months. I think I had the wrong image of her in my mind,' said Mom.

'What do you mean by that?' I interrupted.

'Please listen to me first,' she continued, 'I had a wrong impression of her in my mind. I never thought that she would be so responsible towards her family. I know you might not understand what I am about to say next. The fact is that she took the right decision for her family. She lost her father at an early age as a result of which she had to take on additional responsibilities. Just think once of what you would expect from your sister if she were in Riya's place? Think over it and then react.'

I didn't say anything but left. I went to my room. I saw her gift which was kept on my table. A cute soft toy which she had gifted me. I went near the table and kissed that soft toy. *I didn't notice the last glimpse of your smile before going away. I can't even feel the last kiss. If I could bring back time...*

Now there is a big wall between us. And with every passing hour, it seems like another brick is being cemented on that wall. Try hard as I may, I can't get through it. Someone else took my place in her paradise and closed the doors of her heart. Now, I'm again the stranger she once knew.

With each passing day, I wished for her return. Whenever my phone rang, I wished it was her. Whenever someone touched me from behind, I turned with the hope of that person being her. But it never happened. I don't know how she could forget everything so easily. Can two years of memories be deleted so easily? Not for me at least.

Out of sheer desperation, I tried calling her cell phone one last time and this time the IVR replied, 'Please check the number you have dialled.'

She changed her number! I almost gave up on my search for her.

You should have at least met me once. You should have told me where you were going. You should have at least consulted me once. Jaan, I would have never stopped you. I loved you. I love you even today, I told myself.

I couldn't take it any more and finally opened a beer bottle and drank to my misery. Mohit, seeing that I was heavily drunk, called Sameer and Sonam too. He took me to his house and told me to rest.

'You had promised Riya something, have you forgotten those promises?' Mohit said.

'Which promises are you talking about? Those promises which never meant anything to her? Those promises which she broke within a fraction of a second? Which promises, Mohit?' I shouted as loud as I could. It was the alcohol talking for me.

'Stop it. You very well understand her situation. Keep your hopes alive. By God's grace if some miracle happens, she will return,' said Sameer.

Everything after that passed in a blur. I crashed on the hard floor of Mohit's bedroom, feeling the darkness around engulf me.

An Undelivered Message

It was a lazy Sunday morning. A morning without love. A morning without Riya. I checked my cell phone, I checked my messages, I checked my Facebook account, and I even checked my mail for any signs of Riya. There were none!

I still dwell upon the sweet kisses, the smile that gave me life and keep hoping that I will find you somewhere, before that feeling melts away forever. You have been my strongest emotion, my deepest thought, my sweetest dream, my meaning, my love, my paradise. I wish I could hold you right now in my arms just for one last moment, as I did before.

I wanted to spend time with my memories and give life to my hopes. I decided to switch off my mobile and just roam around the city. The sun was shining brightly. Every morning as the sun rises in the sky, it sets in my heart. I wanted to come out of the darkness and move into the shine of hope. As I drove my bike around the city, I relived the moments and the memories of those lanes. Those days would never come back, but at least the memories of those days brought a smile on my face. Riya was nowhere around yet all around me.

She never tried to contact me again, even though I am still waiting for her one last call. I drove my bike from Navi Mumbai. As I crossed the lane near her apartment where I used to drop her from office, I stopped my bike and stared at that corner aimlessly. I could see nothing but smoke and dust around that corner.

I still keep looking at the places where you would wait for the office cab. You no longer wait there, but I am still on the other side of the same road. I never stopped loving you; I don't think I will ever.

I reached Grant Lane. I parked my bike and sat on the same bench where we started our journey towards life. It reminded me of her yellow top and black jeans, which were one of my favourites. I could feel her sitting beside me, pulling my cheeks. I could feel her playing with my hair. I switched on my mobile and I went to her last message, which said,

Whenever you feel alone, just close your eyes and I would run through your mind. I may not be happy away from you, but I would live my life through your eyes.

I closed my eyes and saw her in your wedding sari. I saw her making tinkling sound of bangles with both her wrists in front of my face. I abruptly opened my eyes just to see a vast lawn in front of me. She was nowhere around.

Tears rolled down my face and fell onto the screen of my mobile, which still had her message opened. I wiped the teardrops from my screen and could see the message, which displayed,

*I wanted to tell you so many things, which I never said.
I wanted to tell you that I may not be with you but the
truth is I may never forget you my entire life. You have
made a deep impact on my life.*

What was it that changed her mind? She never
thought of consulting me even once. She never thought
of asking me how I would feel if she suddenly took
off... All that time I thought I knew her, when really, I
was blind. *Still, I love you and I can never hate you. Even
though you hurt me, I can't let you go.*

*Kasam ki Kasam hai Kasam se, humko pyaar hai sirf
tumse, ab ye pyaar na hoga phir humse...*

My phone kept ringing. I wanted to avoid it, but
since it was Sameer, I couldn't ignore it. I took the call.

'Where the hell have you been since morning? Mohit
and I have been trying your cell phone all day long. I
hope you are alive,' yelled Sameer.

'That's the problem. I am still alive even though I
truly wish I were dead. Anyway, please leave me alone
for a while, guys,' I kept the phone without informing
him where I was.

I moved from that place. I cruised my way to old
Mumbai through Chembur. I reached Bandra. I got
down from the bike and bought a packet of cigarettes.
As I sat down on Bandstand, I lit a cigarette.

I tried to send a message on Riya's cell phone.

*My love, my sweet Riya, I look back at the years that
we shared together, how amazing my time with you was.
Sometimes it breaks my heart to go that far back down*

the road and be reminded of how much I loved you; how much we loved each other. I remember the feelings you gave me whenever I was around you. I have never felt a love so magnificent than what I had in my heart for you. Where have you gone without telling me? Everywhere I look, I see your name, and I find myself getting angry because it only reminds me of the painful truth that I cannot be with you. How could two people who felt they could never live without each other, move apart so easily? How can a love that was meant to last, crumble right before our very eyes? What happened to our love... What happened to us? I only wish things in life were simpler so that I could be with you. I will love you forever.

Message delivery failed!

Helpless, depressed, and broken, I just left from that place. It was the same place where we shared one of the earliest kisses.

I reached home and closed the door of my room. After some time, there was a knock at my door. I opened it to find Sameer looking at me with all the anger available in the world. I was in no mood to talk with him. Neither had I attended Mohit's calls.

'What is your problem in life? You can't live for others? Do your family and friends mean anything to you?' Sameer shouted at me.

'Sameer, what do you expect from me? Life without Riya is pointless,' I said with dejection.

'If you love her so much, why don't you remember what she said? Just because she is not with you doesn't means she doesn't love you. She told you that she wants to live her life through your eyes. You are hurting her each day without realizing it,' said Sameer.

'What do you expect from me?' I replied.

'I don't expect anything. But just stop hurting others as much as you are hurting yourself. Wherever Riya is, I know she must be thinking of you at this moment and if she senses that you are ruining your life by not doing anything productive, she would be very upset,' Sameer patted my back and left saying that he would come by in the night after having dinner.

I gave a thought to Sameer's views and recapped the message and Mom's suggestion. It was hard to digest the fact that Riya couldn't be with me anymore. I missed those midnight conversations and I missed how Riya would make me laugh when I would be frustrated after a hard day's work. *I want to be with you but whether you are millions of miles away or just beside me, I still don't know. I wish you would call just to ask about my day. It would make things so much better if I could hear your voice.*

I guess I can't complain too much. It wasn't your choice. You were always there for me through both the good times and the bad. You were always there to laugh with me, or to help me when I was sad. It's not that I pity you, but I'll admit your life's been tough. I just wish that physically, I could be there when things got tough for you. Maybe even today you love me.

I realized that love should not be bounded with promises. Love should be set free with no restrictions. There are no promises in love, there is only magic in love. It's the long wait... The magic to wait for your love.

Love is like life, where you don't find smooth roads, where you don't achieve goals so easily. You have to struggle for it, but when you don't stop living you life, why should one stop loving someone?

Sameer came again at night as he had promised, bringing along a bottle of vodka with him.

'Did you give it a serious thought?' Sameer asked as he handed me a shot of vodka.

'Ya, I did. I know Riya was not wrong. She loved me and wanted to marry me. It was she who convinced me to get married secretly. But then situations changed and suddenly she was forced to change her decisions. There must have been some kind of external pressure on her that made her leave her home and shift somewhere else. Otherwise she would have definitely told me,' I said gulping the drink down in one shot.

God alone knew how much I loved her, how much she meant to me. If I am in such deep pain, what must be her condition?

You loved me more than I could imagine. Remember those sweet ice creams? I now understand why they tasted so good. It was just eating it with you that made them taste sweet. Now that you are gone, their sweetness has gone too.

Sameer got up and went to my table to bring the bottle of vodka.

'What kind of a diary is this?' he asked me.

'Nothing, just forget about it. Leave it be,' I said.

He didn't listen to me and opened the diary. I was in no mood to get up and steal it from him. I let him read it. After some time I went to sleep drugged by the alcohol. The next morning when I got up, Sameer was there to greet me at the breakfast table.

'I read your diary. You write well. All your memories associated with Riya—from the day you first met her to the day she mysteriously disappeared,' he said.

I kept quiet and just sipped the tea. I was still hungover. He continued speaking.

'You should try to get this diary published by changing the name of the protagonist. I am telling you this because if your book is published and Riya reads it, then she might come back to you. But again, that is just my opinion,' he said.

'Crazy, fucking crazy you are. I think you have a hangover. Kindly go home and sleep. You need rest. You are just uttering crap right now. I ignored the useless topic. I told him to leave and shut the door. When I shut the door, I thought to myself, *Was it good enough to be published?* Errr… I stand nowhere. Forget it! I again thought about it and opened my diary. I read a few pages of it.

Fuck, no! Forget it!

Today…

Today we are not together, today we are living our own lives; but does that mean that we have stopped loving each other? Absolutely not. You're a very special soul in my life and you will always continue to be. I love you with all my being and I accept that we are now travelling down different paths in our lives, but my love for you will always remain constant and our past will be relived in my dreams. Though our roads are different, our paths may cross and maybe someday in the future, our roads will meet and we will travel down the same path once again, until then my sweet love ... In my heart is where you always reside.

Love is pain. Love is pure. Love is sacrifice!

Epilogue

Log har manzil ko mushkil samajhte hai,
Maine har mushkil ko manzil samjha hai,
Log dil ko dard samajhte hai,
Maine dard ko dil samjha hai...

When you love someone, you love that person as a whole—you love them for both their strengths and their weaknesses... I did nothing different. Somewhere Riya still belongs to me, and even if today we are not together, she still happens to be my love.

If you believe in love, you should never curse your love for not being with you today. Rise in love, and make them proud of you for loving them.

What happened next?

After a few months, I completed writing my manuscript. I called everyone to inform them that I had finally completed my story. I never thought I would do that. I still couldn't believe it. Mohit, Sonam, and Sameer were equally shocked when they read it. We searched for some publishers in Mumbai but absolutely no one entertained me. Forget about reading the script, they never even gave me a second glance. I was rejected by most of the big publishing houses in Mumbai just because I didn't have a godfather.

I wanted my Riya back; I wanted to prove myself to her. I sent my script to one of the finest publishing houses in India. To my surprise, they sent me a mail within a month saying that my script was under consideration.

Mohit and Sameer were on cloud nine when I told them we have moved one step closer towards Riya. One step closer in search of Riya. Finally, after some days when I opened my mail, I had a mail from the very same publisher in my inbox.

Fuck… This is unbelievable! I shouted like a little kid who had been given his dream toy in his hands.

I called Mohit up and told him that there was a big surprise waiting for him in his mailbox, I called Sameer and Sonam too.

They saw their mails and everyone jumped with excitement. I was in my room when I called my parents in the room. I showed them the cover page on my PC.

'You are drunk? You didn't get anyone else to fool around. Do your work,' my Mom replied.

'Mom, I am serious. This is the cover page of my novel, *Few Things Left Unsaid*. Trust me!' I convinced her.

She did not believe me until she heard me talking with the publishers. She hugged me and congratulated me on my achievement. But my real reason for writing the novel still remains the same after all these years. I am still in search of Riya…

Riya, I don't know where you are today. But wherever you are, I know you miss me more than I do. I know you still love me. Riya, you had told me once that you wanted me to achieve something extraordinary in life and make you feel proud of me. Well, I think you will be very proud of me today.

July 13, 2011. It was the launch day of my debut novel. Mumbai was once again under a terrorist attack. There had been three bomb blasts within a span of thirty minutes, with the first one just one minute before my launch at seven in the evening. The launch was very successful and the high sales made my book a national bestseller within a month of its release. I still found no sign of you. I still waited for that one last phone call from you. I remember being called for an on-air interview on Radio Mirchi 98.3 FM, Mumbai studio.

'Aditya, is this your true love story? You have mentioned in the book that it's your true story,' the RJ had asked me on air.

'Absolutely! Everyone falls in love at least once in his or her life. Everyone has memories. I decided to pen them down and make them eternal.'

'What inspired you to pen down your own story?' The RJ asked one more question.

'Riya! Who else could it be? I don't know where she is today. I hope wherever she is, she is reading my novel and who knows, maybe she is listening to this interview as well.'

'That's the spirit! A 22-year-old guy wrote his love story for all to read. Such an act needs courage and Mumbai appreciates it. You have described and explored Mumbai in *Few Things Left Unsaid*. I loved it. It's hot,' the RJ said and we finished our interview.

The interview became such a big hit that I was flooded with congratulatory calls. But the call I wanted to receive the most never came.

My book became a national bestseller within a few months of its release. Everything seemed like a dream come true.

I got a call from Mohit. He told me that I had been invited to the Ahmedabad film festival as a special guest.

'You must be kidding! Why would they call me?' I asked him.

'Dude, I told the organizers about your novel. One of them even read it and said that he was inspired by it.'

I packed my bags and reached Ahmedabad—the place where Riya and I had vacationed together. But this time, I was all alone with just my memories for company. When I reached Ahmedabad, I was flooded with fans asking for autographs. The majority of my fans, I noticed, were girls. I thanked my fans for their love and support. I moved towards one of my friend's home when a guy approached me.

'Dude, you have set a wrong example for true lovers. You should have waited for Riya. You shouldn't have written the novel.'

I smiled and replied, 'I am sorry to have hurt your feelings. But you see, I didn't have any option and I went with what my heart told me to do. But if that seemed to have offended you, then I am really sorry.'

'No dude, I respect you. Your courage and selfbelief is worth appreciating. However, for those who need to move on in their life, you would set a bad example. They would do something similar to this. Don't you think so?'

'I have never stopped anyone from moving ahead in life and will never do so. Even I have moved on. Loving someone and waiting for someone to come back in your life doesn't mean you should forget about others around you. If your love is true, that person will ultimately come back to you. But in the meantime, you should not stop living your life. You should instead live for them and do whatever you want in your life thinking of them in your heart. Love is not about two people being together for their entire life. It's about the sacrifices you make for each other, knowing you can't be with them for your entire life. But still you hope for it.'

He hugged me and and thanked me for giving him a fuller perspective on it. I reached the film festival event. By the end of the event, I got up from my seat and turned to move towards the exit. There I saw a beautiful girl who resembled Riya in every sense. Her black eyeliner, her fair skin, her tiny nose, and her perfect jaw line—my God, she looked so much like Riya!.. She looked at me. She was wearing a long skirt with a black top over it. Her skin glowed in the spotlight of the stage. She kept staring at me while I tried to look the other way.

'Let's move. Our car is waiting outside,' Mohit said while another friend waited backstage.

Mohit looked at me and saw me looking at her. He looked at her when her eyes were still searching for me. We didn't speak a word. We didn't say anything to each other. I moved down the stage. I walked towards the exit. I turned to see that her eyes were still on me. I smiled.

She resembled Riya. However, she wasn't Riya. From somewhere, from some corner of the world I wished I could see Riya for once. She still holds a special place in my heart. I love you. I love you, Riya.

A person lost in love can win anything in this world. Just because he has nothing to lose. He will only rise now!

Maybe it's just an act. Maybe you still do think of me often, in stealing moments, or at night when you can't fall asleep; wondering if I am wondering too.

If it were not for you, my love, this book would not have been written. I am still searching for you.

Acknowledgements

First, let me thank the masses of India who turned my first novel, *Few Things Left Unsaid* (2011), into a bestseller within three months of its release. This acknowledgement itself would not have been written if it were not for the love of these people. I owe my success to them.

Thank you, my readers, for all the support. You all mean a lot to me. (But only those who liked it!)

I had thanked a few people in my first book and would like to thank them again just because they did nothing! These include Rohan, Clera, Pratiksha, Tushar, Viraj, and Suhas Sonawane. The last time I thanked them (which was in my previous book), the book worked.

Also a big thank you to Saurabh, Amit, Mrunmayee, Sunita, Mom, Dad, and my sister, Shweta Nagarkar, for their humble support through it all, even when I used to get hyper at times. I love you all.

Thank you to my grandparents, Divakar Palimkar and Sulbha Palimkar, for your constant support.

I would also like to make a few special mentions: Shalini for being the warmest reader, Diksha for the sweet girl in her, Ananya Kapoor and Karan Bajaj for their support, Prashant and Zankrut for all the promotions, and Abhinay, Shruti, Ananya, Kasturi, Roshni, Nidhi, Nikita, Snehanka, and Nithesh for being so loyal to me throughout my journey.

Thanks to all my loyal Facebook fans for your constant support and feedback.

I would like to thank the electronic media and print media who extended support to my work through their network. Special thanks to RJ Jeeturaaj and the entire Radio Mirchi team in Mumbai for all their love. I would also like to thank Prakash Bal Joshi and Soumitra Pote for the first ever article on me in print media. I am overwhelmed by their support.

How can I forget to thank that one special person without which the book would not have been written in the first place? Many thanks, my love, for giving me the strength I need and for making me believe that I can achieve anything. I don't know if we will ever cross paths in the future, but for now, I just want to thank you for all the love through the years we were together and for all the memories that were born out of it.

Thank you also to all the editors and the publicity team at Random House India for keeping faith in me and for all the patience and love. They were with me whenever I needed (which was once in every few hours).

Lastly, thanks to Milee Ashwarya and Gurveen Chadha from Random House India for putting up with all my crazy antics. You both rock!

I am extremely sorry if I have missed a few names, but each and every one of you holds a special place in my heart.

A Note on the Author

S udeep Nagarkar is the bestselling author of *Few Things Left Unsaid.*

He has a degree in Electronics Engineering from Mumbai. His books are inspired from real-life incidents. He never dreamed of becoming an author, but turned into one for his love. Apart from writing, Sudeep is a music enthusiast and loves to spend time with his friends. He resides in Mumbai.

Connect with Sudeep on www.facebook.com/sudeep.nagarkar, email him at sudeepnagarkar@gmail.com, or visit his website, www.sudeepnagarkar.com, to know more.